Betty's Bright Idea;
Deacon Pitkin's Farm;
and The First Christmas
of New England

Harriet Beecher Stowe

Contents

BETTY'S BRIGHT IDEA;
DEACON PITKIN'S FARM;
AND THE FIRST C
HRISTMAS OF
NEW ENGLAND

BY

Harriet Beecher Stowe

BETTY'S BRIGHT IDEA.

"When He ascended up on high, He led captivity captive, and gave gifts unto men."--Eph. iv. 8.

Some say that ever, 'gainst that season comes Wherein our Saviour's birth is celebrate, The bird of dawning singeth all night long. And then, they say, no evil spirit walks; The nights are wholesome; then no planets strike, No fairy takes, no witch hath power to charm,-- So hallowed and so gracious is the time.

And this holy time, so hallowed and so gracious, was settling down over the great roaring, rattling, seething life-world of New York in the good year 1875. Who does not feel its on-coming in the shops and streets, in the festive air of trade and business, in the thousand garnitures by which every store hangs out triumphal banners and solicits you to buy something for a Christmas gift? For it is the peculiarity of all this array of prints, confectionery, dry goods, and manufactures of all kinds, that their bravery and splendor at Christmas tide is all to seduce you into generosity, and importune you to give something to others. It says to you, "The dear God gave you an unspeakable gift; give you a lesser gift to your brother!"

Do we ever think, when we walk those busy, bustling streets, all alive with Christmas shoppers, and mingle with the rushing tides that throng and jostle through the stores, that unseen spirits may be hastening to and fro along those same ways bearing Christ's Christmas gifts to men-- gifts whose value no earthly gold or gems can represent?

Yet, on this morning of the day before Christmas, were these Shining Ones, moving to and fro with the crowd, whose faces were loving and serene as the invisible stars, whose robes took no defilement from the spatter and the rush of earth, whose coming and going was still as the falling snow-flakes. They entered houses without ringing door-bells, they passed through apartments without opening doors, and everywhere they were bearing Christ's Christmas presents, and silently offering them to whoever would open their souls to receive. Like themselves, their gifts were invisible--incapable of weight and measurement in gross earthly scales. To mourners they carried joy; to weary and perplexed hearts, peace; to souls stifling in luxury and self-indulgence they carried that noble discontent that rises to aspiration for higher things. Sometimes they took away an earthly treasure to make room for a heavenly one. They took health, but left resignation and cheerful faith. They took the babe from the dear cradle, but left in its place a heart full of pity for the suffering on earth and a fellowship with the blessed in heaven. Let us follow their footsteps awhile.

SCENE I.

A young girl's boudoir in one of our American palaces of luxury, built after the choicest fancy of the architect, and furnished in all the latest devices of household decoration. Pictures, statuettes, and every form of *bijouterie* make the room a miracle of beauty, and the little princess of all sits in an easy chair before the fire, and thus revolves with herself:

"O, dear me! Christmas is a bore! Such a rush and crush in the streets, such a jam in the shops, and then *such* a fuss thinking up presents for everybody! All for nothing, too; for nobody Wants anything. I'm sure *I* don't. I'm surfeited now with pictures and jewelry, and bon-bon boxes, and little china dogs and cats--and all these things that get so thick you can't move without upsetting some of them. There's papa, he don't want anything. He never uses any of my Christmas presents when I get them; and mamma, she has every earthly thing I can think of, and said the other day she did hope nobody'd give her any more worsted work! Then Aunt Maria and Uncle John, they don't want the things I give them; they have more than they know what to do with, now. All the boys say they don't want any more cigar cases or slippers, or smoking caps. Oh, dear!"

Here the Shining Ones came and stood over the little lady, and looked down on her with faces of pity, which seemed blent with a serene and half-amused indulgence. It was a heavenly amusement, such as that with which mothers listen to the foolish-wise prattle of children just learning to talk.

As the grave, sweet eyes rested tenderly on her, the girl somehow grew graver, leaned back in her chair, and sighed a little.

"I wish I knew how to be better!" she said to herself. "I remember last Sunday's text, 'It is more blessed to give than to receive.' That must mean something! Well, isn't there something, too, in the Bible about not giving to your rich neighbors that can give again, but giving to the poor that cannot recompense you? I don't know any poor people. Papa says there are very few deserving poor people. Well, for the matter of that, there aren't many ***deserving rich*** people. I, for example, how much do I ***deserve*** to have all these nice things? I'm no better than the poor shop-girls that go trudging by in the cold at six o'clock in the morning-- ugh! it makes me shiver to think of it. I know if I had to do that *I* shouldn't be good at all. Well, I'd like to give to poor people, if I knew any."

At this moment the door opened and the maid entered.

"Betty, do you know any poor people I ought to get things for, this Christmas?"

"Poor folks is always plenty, miss," said Betty.

"O yes, of course, beggars; but I mean people that I could do something for besides just give cold victuals or money. I don't know where to hunt them up, and should be afraid to go if I did. O dear! it's no use. I'll give it up."

"Why, Miss Florence, that 'ud be too bad, afther bein' that good in yer heart, to let the poor folks alone for fear of goin' to them. But ye needn't do that, for, now I think of it, there's John Morley's wife."

"What, the gardener father turned off for drinking?"

"The same, miss. Poor boy, he's not so bad, and he's got a wife and two as pretty children as ever you see."

"I always liked John," said the young lady. "But papa is so strict about some things! He says he never will keep a man a day if he finds out that he drinks."

She was quite silent for a minute, and then broke out:

"I don't care; it's a good idea! I say, Betty, do you know where John's wife lives?"

"Yes, miss, I've been there often."

"Well, then, this afternoon I'll go with you and see if I can do anything for them."

SCENE II.

An attic room, neat and clean, but poorly furnished; a bed and a trundle- bed, a small cooking-stove, a shelf with a few dishes, one or two chairs and stools, a pale, thin woman working on a vest.

Her face is anxious; her thin hands tremble with weakness, and now and then, as she works, quiet tears drop, which she wipes quickly. Poor people cannot afford to shed tears; it takes time and injures eyesight.

This is John Morley's wife. This morning he has risen and gone out in a desperate mood. "No use to try," he says. "Didn't I go a whole year and never touch a drop? And now just because I fell once I'm kicked out! No use to try. When a fellow once trips, everybody gives him a kick. Talk about love of Christ! Who believes it? Don't see much love of Christ where I go. Your Christians hit a fellow that's down as hard as anybody. It's everybody for himself and devil take the hindmost. Well, I'll trudge up to the Brooklyn Navy Yard and see if they'll take me on there--if they won't I might as well go to sea, or to the devil," and out he flings.

"Mamma!" says a little voice, "what are we going to have for our Christmas?"

It is a little girl, with soft curly hair and bright, earnest eyes, that speaks.

A sturdy little fellow of four presses up to the mother's knee and repeats the question, "Sha'n't we have a Christmas, mother?"

It overcomes the poor woman; she leans forward and breaks into sobbing,-- a tempest of sorrow, long suppressed, that shakes her weak frame as she thinks that her husband is out of work, desperate, discouraged, and tempted of the devil, that the rent is falling due, and only the poor pay of her needle to meet it with. In one of those quick flashes which concentrate through the imagination the sorrows of years, she seems to see her little home broken up, her husband in the gutter, her children turned into the street. At this moment there goes up from her heart a despairing cry, such as a poor, hunted, tired-out creature gives when brought to the last gasp of endurance. It was like the shriek of the hare when the hounds are upon it. She clasps her hands and cries out, "O my God, help me."

There was no voice of any that answered; there was no sound of foot-fall on the staircase; no one entered the door; and yet that agonized cry had reached the heart it was meant for. The Shining Ones were with her; they stood, with faces full of tenderness, beaming down upon her; they brought her a Christmas gift from Christ--the gift of trust. She knew not from whence came the courage and rest that entered her soul; but while her little ones stood wondering and silent, she turned and drew to herself her well-worn Bible. Hands that she did not see guided her as she turned the pages, and pointed the words: ***He shall deliver the needy when he crieth; the poor also and him that hath no helper. He shall spare the poor and needy, and shall save the souls of the needy. He shall redeem their soul from deceit and violence, and precious shall their blood be in his sight.***

She laid down her poor wan cheek on the merciful old book, as on her mother's breast, and gave up all the tangled skein of life into the hands of Infinite Pity. There seemed a consoling presence in the room, and her tired heart found rest.

She wiped away her tears, kissed her children, and smiled upon them. Then she rose, gathered up her finished work, and attired herself to go forth and carry it back to the shop.

"Mother," said the children softly, "they are dressing the church, and the gates are open, and people are going in and out; mayn't we play there by the church?"

The mother looked out on the ivy-grown walls of the church, with its flocks of twittering sparrows, and said:

"Yes, my little birds; you may play there if you'll be very good and quiet."

The mother had only her small, close attic room for her darlings, and to satisfy all their childish desire for variety and motion, she had only the refuge of the streets. She was a decent, godly woman, and the bold manners and evil words of street vagrants were terrible to her; and so, when the church gates were open for daily morning and evening prayers, she had often begged the sexton to let her little ones come in and hear the singing, and wander hand in hand around the old church walls. He was a kindly old man, and the children, stealing round like two still, bright-eyed little mice, had gained upon his heart, and he made them welcome there. It gave the mother a feeling of protection to have them play near the church, as if it were a father's house.

So she put on their little hoods and tippets, and led them forth, and saw them into the yard; and as she looked to the old gray church, with its rustling ivy bowers and flocks of birds, her heart swelled within her. "Yea, the sparrow hath found a house and the swallow a nest where she may lay her young, even thine altars, O Lord of hosts, my king and my God!" And the Shining Ones walking with her said, "Fear not; ye are of more value than many sparrows."

SCENE III.

The little ones went gayly into the yard. They had been scared by their mother's tears; but she had smiled again, and that had made all right with them. The sun was shining brightly, and they were on the sunny side of the old church, and they laughed and chirped and chittered to each other as merrily as the little birds in the ivy boughs.

The old sexton came to the side door and threw out an armful of refuse greens, and then stopped a moment and nodded kindly at them.

"May we play with them, please, sir?" said the little Elsie, looking up with great reverence.

"Oh, yes, to be sure; these are done with--they are no good now."

"Oh, Tottie!" cried Elsie, rapturously, "just think, he says we may play with all these. Why, here's ever and ever so much green, enough to play house. Let's play build a house for father and mother."

"I'm going to build a big house for 'em when I grow up," said Tottie, "and I mean to have glass bead windows in it."

Tottie had once had presented to him a box of colored glass beads to string, and he could think of nothing finer in the future than unlimited glass beads.

Meanwhile, his sister began planting pine branches upright in the snow, to make her house.

"You see we can make believe there are windows and doors and a roof," she said, "and it's just as good. Now, let's make believe there is a bed in this corner, and we will lie down to sleep."

And Tottie obediently couched himself in the allotted corner and shut his eyes very hard, though after a moment he remarked that the snow got into his neck.

"You must play it isn't snow--play it's feathers," said Elsie.

"But I don't like it," persisted Tottie, "it don't feel a bit like feathers."

"Oh, well, then," said Elsie, accommodating herself to circumstances, "let's play get up now and I'll get breakfast."

Just now the door opened again, and the sexton began sweeping the refuse out of the church. There were bits of ivy and holly, and ruffles of ground-pine, and lots of bright red berries that came flying forth into the yard, and the children screamed for joy. "O Tottie!" "O Elsie!" "Only see how many pretty things--lots and lots!"

The sexton stood and looked and laughed as he saw the little ones so eager for the scraps and remnants.

"Don't you want to come in and see the church?" he said. "It's all done now, and a brave sight it is. You may come in."

They tipped in softly, with large bright, wondering eyes. The light through the stained glass windows fell blue and crimson and yellow on the pillars all ruffled with ground-pine and brightened with scarlet bitter- sweet berries, and there were stars and crosses and mottoes in green all through the bowery aisles, while the organist, hid in a thicket of verdure, was practicing softly, and sweet voices sung:

"Hark! the herald angels sing Glory to the new-born King."

The little ones wandered up and down the long aisles in a dream of awe and wonder. "Hush, Tottie!" said Elsie when he broke into an eager exclamation, "don't make a noise. I do believe it's something like heaven," she said, under her breath.

They made the course of the church and came round by the door again, where the sexton stood smiling on them.

"You can find lots of pretty Christmas greens out there," he said, pointing to the door; "perhaps your folks would like to have some."

"Oh, thank you, sir," exclaimed. Elsie, rapturously. "Oh, Tottie, only think! Let's gather a good lot and go home and dress our room for Christmas. Oh, ***won't*** mother be astonished when she comes home, we'll make it so pretty!"

And forthwith the children began gathering into their little aprons wreaths of ground-pine, sprigs of holly, and twigs of crimson bitter- sweet. The sexton, seeing their zeal, brought out to them a little cross, fancifully made of red alder-berries and pine.

Then he said, "A lady took that down to put up a bigger one, and she gave it to me; you may have it if you want it."

"Oh, how beautiful," said Elsie. "How glad I am to have this for mother! When she comes back she won't know our room; it will be as fine as the church."

Soon the little gleaners were toddling off out of the yard--moving masses of green with all that their aprons and their little hands could carry.

The sexton looked after them. "Take heed that ye despise not these little ones," he said to himself, "for in heaven their angels--"

A ray of tenderness fell on the old man's head; it was from the Shining One who watched the children. He thought it was an afternoon sunbeam. His heart grew gentle and peaceful, and his thoughts went far back to a distant green grove where his own little one was sleeping. "Seems to me I've loved all little ones ever since," he said, thinking far back to the Christmas week when his lamb was laid to rest. "Well, she shall not return to me, but I shall go to her." The smile of the Shining One made a warm glow in his heart, which followed him all the way home.

The children had a merry time dressing the room. They stuck good big bushes of pine in each window; they put a little ruffle of ground-pine round mother's Bible, and they fastened the beautiful red cross up over the table, and they stuck sprigs of pine or holly into every crack that could be made, by fair means or foul, to accept it, and they were immensely satisfied and delighted. Tottie insisted on hanging up his string of many-colored beads in the window to imitate the effect of the stained glass of the great church window.

"It looks pretty when the light comes through," he remarked; and Elsie admitted that they might play they were painted windows, with some show of propriety. When everything had been stuck somewhere, Elsie swept the floor, and made up a fire, and put on the tea-kettle, to have everything ready to strike mother favorably on her return.

SCENE IV.

A freezing, bright, cold afternoon. "Cold as Christmas!" say cheery voices, as the crowds rush to and fro into shops and stores, and come out with hands full of presents.

"Yes, cold as Christmas," says John Morley. "I should think so! Cold enough for a fellow that can't get in anywhere--that nobody wants and nobody helps! I should think so."

John had been trudging all day from point to point, only to hear the old story: times were hard, work was dull, nobody wanted him, and he felt morose and surly--out of humor with himself and with everybody else.

It is true that his misfortunes were from his own fault; but that consideration never makes a man a particle more patient or good-natured-- indeed, it is an additional bitterness in his cup. John was an Englishman. When he first landed in New York from the old country, he had been wild and dissipated and given to drinking. But by his wife's earnest entreaties he had been persuaded to sign the temperance pledge, and had gone on prosperously keeping it for a year. He had a good place and good wages, and all went well with him till in an evil hour he met some of his former boon-companions, and was induced to have a social evening with them.

In the first half hour of that evening were lost the fruits of the whole year's self-denial and self-control. He was not only drunk that night, but he went off for a fortnight, and was drunk night after night, and came back to find that his master had discharged him in indignation. John thinks this over bitterly, as he thuds about in the cold and calls himself a fool.

Yet, if the truth must be confessed, John had not much "sense of sin," so called. He looked on himself as an unfortunate and rather ill-used man, for had he not tried very hard to be good, and gone a great while against the stream of evil inclination? and now, just for one yielding, he was pitched out of place, and everybody was turned against him! He thought this was hard measure. Didn't everybody hit wrong sometimes? Didn't rich fellows have their wine, and drink a little too much now and then? Yet nobody was down on ***them***.

"It's only because I'm poor," said John. "Poor folks' sins are never pardoned. There's my good wife--poor girl!" and John's heart felt as if it were breaking, for he was an affectionate creature, and loved his wife and babies, and in his deepest consciousness he knew that he was the one at fault. We have heard much about the sufferings of the wives and children of men who are overtaken with drink; but what is not so well understood is the sufferings of the men themselves in their sober moments, when they feel that they are becoming a curse to all that are dearest to them. John's very soul was wrung within him to think of the misery he had brought on his wife and children--the greater miseries that might be in store for them. He was faint of heart; he was tired; he had eaten nothing for hours, and on ahead he saw a drinking saloon. Why shouldn't he go and take one good drink, and then pitch off a ferry-boat into the East River, and so end the whole miserable muddle of life altogether?

John's steps were turning that way, when one of the Shining Ones, who had watched him all day, came nearer and took his hand. He felt no touch; but at that moment there darted into his soul a thought of his mother, long dead, and he stopped irresolute, then turned to walk another way. The hand that was guiding him led him to turn a corner, and his curiosity was excited by a stream of people who seemed to be pressing into a building. A distant sound of singing was heard as he drew nearer, and soon he found himself passing with the multitude into a great prayer-meeting. The music grew more distinct as he went in. A man was singing in clear, penetrating tones:

"What means this eager, anxious throng, Which moves with busy haste along; These wondrous gatherings day by day; What means this strange commotion, say? In accents hushed the throng reply, 'Jesus of Nazareth passeth by!'"

John had but a vague idea of religion, yet something in the singing affected him; and, weary and footsore and heartsore as he was, he sank into a seat and listened with absorbed attention:

"Jesus! 'tis he who once below Man's pathway trod in toil and woe; And burdened ones where'er he came Brought out their sick and deaf and lame. The blind rejoiced to hear the cry, 'Jesus of Nazareth passeth by!'

"Ho, all ye heavy-laden, come! Here's pardon, comfort, rest, and home. Ye wanderers from a Father's face, Return, accept his proffered grace. Ye tempted ones, there's refuge nigh-- 'Jesus of Nazareth passeth by!'"

A plain man, who spoke the language of plain working-men, now arose and read from his Bible the words which the angel of old spoke to the shepherds of Bethlehem:

"Fear not, for behold, I bring you tidings of great joy, which shall be to all people, for unto you is born this day a Saviour, which is Christ the Lord."

The man went on to speak of this with an intense practical earnestness that soon made John feel as if *he*, individually, were being talked to; and the purport of the speech was this: that God had sent to him, John Morley, a Saviour to save him from his sins, to lift him above his weakness, to help him overcome his bad habits; that His name was called Jesus, because he shall save his people *from their sins*. John listened with a strange new thrill. This was what he needed--a Friend, all-powerful, all-pitiful, who would undertake for him and help him to overcome himself--for he sorely felt how weak he was. Here was a Friend that could have compassion on the ignorant and them that were out of the way. The thought brought tears to his eyes and a glow of hope to his heart. What if He *would* help him? for deep down in John's heart, worse than cold or hunger or weariness, was the dreadful conviction that he was a doomed man, that he should drink again as he had drunk, and never come to good, but fall lower and lower, and drag all who loved him down with him.

And was this mighty Saviour given to him?

"Yes," cried the man who was speaking; "to *you;* to you, who have lost name and place; to you, that nobody cares for; to you, who have been down in the gutter. God has sent you a Saviour to take you up out of the mud and mire, to wash you clean, to give you strength to overcome your sins, and lead you home to his blessed kingdom. This is the glad tidings of great joy that the angels brought on the first Christmas day. Christ was *God's Christmas gift* to a poor, lost world, and you may have him now, to-day. He may be your own Saviour--yours as much as if there were no other one on earth to be saved. He is looking for you to-day, coming after you, seeking you; he calls you by me. Oh, accept him now!"

There was a deep breathing of suppressed emotion as the speaker sat down, a pause of solemn stillness.

A faint strain of music was heard, and the singer began singing a pathetic ballad of a lost sheep and of the Shepherd going forth to seek it:

"There were ninety and nine that safely lay
  In the shelter of the fold,
But one was out on the hills away,
  Far off from the gates of gold--
Away on the mountains wild and bare,
Away from the tender Shepherd's care.

"'Lord, Thou hast here Thy ninety and nine;
  Are they not enough for Thee?'
But the Shepherd made answer: "Tis of mine
  Has wandered away from me;
And although the road be rough and steep
I go to the desert to find my sheep.'"

John heard with an absorbed interest. All around him were eager listeners, breathless, leaning forward with intense attention. The song went on:

"But none of the ransomed ever knew
  How deep were the waters crossed;
Nor how dark was the night that the Lord went through
  Ere He found His sheep that was lost.
Out in the desert He heard its cry--
Sick and helpless, and ready to die."

There was a throbbing pathos in the intonation, and the verse floated over the weeping throng; when, after a pause, the strain was taken up triumphantly:

"But all through the mountains thunder-riven,
  And up from the rocky steep,
There rose a cry to the gates of heaven,
  'Rejoice! I have found my sheep!'
And the angels echoed around the throne,

'Rejoice, for the Lord brings back His own!'"

All day long, poor John had felt so lonesome! Nobody cared for him; nobody wanted him; everything was against him; and, worst of all, he had no faith in himself. But here was this Friend, **seeking** him, following him through the cold alleys and crowded streets. In heaven they would be glad to hear that he had become a good man. The thought broke down all his pride, all his bitterness; he wept like a little child; and the Christmas gift of Christ--the sense of a real, present, loving, pitying Saviour--came into his very *soul*.

He went homeward as one in a dream. He passed the drinking-saloon without a thought or wish of drinking. The expulsive force of a new emotion had for the time driven out all temptation. Raised above weakness, he thought only of this Jesus, this Saviour from sin, who he now believed had followed him and found him, and he longed to go home and tell his wife what great things the Lord had done for him.

SCENE V.

Meanwhile a little drama had been acting in John's humble home. His wife had been to the shop that day and come home with the pittance for her work in her hands.

"I'll pay you full price to-day, but we can't pay such prices any longer," the man had said over the counter as he paid her. "Hard times-- work dull--we are cutting down all our work-folks; you'll have to take a third less next time."

"I'll do my best," she said meekly, as she took her bundle of work and turned wearily away, but the invisible arm of the Shining One was round her, and the words again thrilled through her that she had read that morning: "He shall redeem their soul from deceit and violence, and precious shall their blood be in his sight." She saw no earthly helper; she heard none and felt none, and yet her soul was sustained, and she came home in peace.

When she opened the door of her little room she drew back astonished at the sight that presented itself. A brisk fire was roaring in the stove, and the tea-kettle was sputtering and sending out clouds of steam. A table with a white cloth on it was drawn out before the fire, and a new tea set of pure white cups and saucers, with teapot, sugar-bowl, and creamer, complete, gave a festive air to the whole. There were bread, and butter, and ham-sandwiches, and a Christmas cake all frosted, with little blue and red and green candles round it ready to be lighted, and a bunch of hot-house flowers in a pretty little vase in the centre.

A new stuffed rocking-chair stood on one side of the stove, and there sat Miss Florence De Witt, our young princess of Scene First, holding little Elsie in her lap, while the broad, honest countenance of Betty was beaming with kindness down on the delighted face of Tottie. Both children were dressed from head to foot in complete new suits of clothes, and Elsie was holding with tender devotion a fine doll, while Tottie rejoiced in a horse and cart which he was maneuvering under Betty's superintendence.

The little princess had pleased herself in getting up all this tableau. Doing good was a novelty to her, and she plunged into it with the zest of a new amusement. The amazed look of the poor woman, her dazed expressions of rapture and incredulous joy, the shrieks and cries of confused delight with which the little ones met their mother, delighted her more than any scene she had ever witnessed at the opera-- with this added grace, unknown to her, that at this scene the invisible Shining Ones were pleased witnesses.

She had been out with Betty, buying here and there whatever was wanted,-- and what was ***not*** wanted for those who had been living so long without work or money?

She had their little coal-bin filled, and a nice pile of wood and kindlings put behind the stove. She had bought a nice rocking-chair for the mother to rest in. She had dressed the children from head to foot at a ready-made clothing store, and bought them toys to their hearts' desire, while Betty had set the table for a Christmas feast.

And now she said to the poor woman at last:

"I'm so sorry John lost his place at father's. He was so kind and obliging, and I always liked him; and I've been thinking, if you'd get him to sign the pledge over again from Christmas Eve, never to touch another drop, I'll get papa to take him back. I always do get papa to do what I want, and the fact is, he hasn't got anybody that suited him so well since John left. So you tell John that I mean to go surety for him; he certainly won't fail *me*. Tell him *I trust him*." And Miss Florence pulled out a paper wherein, in her best round hand, she had written out again the temperance pledge, and dated it "*Christmas Eve, 1875*."

"Now, you come with John to-morrow morning, and bring this with his name to it, and you'll see what I'll do!" and, with a kiss to the children, the little good fairy departed, leaving the family to their Christmas Eve.

What that Christmas Eve was, when the husband and father came home with the new and softened heart that had been given him, who can say? There were joyful tears and solemn prayers, and earnest vows and purposes of a new life heard by the Shining Ones in the room that night.

"And the angels echoed around the throne, Rejoice! for the Lord brings back his own."

SCENE VI.

"Now, papa, I want you to give me something special to-day, because it's Christmas," said the little princess to her father, as she kissed and wished him "Merry Christmas" next morning.

"What is it, Pussy--half of my kingdom?"

"No, no, papa; not so much as that. It's a little bit of my own way that I want."

"Of course; well, what is it?"

"Well, I want you to take John back again."

Her father's face grew hard.

"Now, please, papa, don't say a word till you have heard me. John was a capital gardener; he kept the green-house looking beautiful; and this Mike that we've got now, he's nothing but an apprentice, and stupid as an owl at that! He'll never do in the world."

"All that is very true," said Mr. De Witt, "but *John drinks*, and I *won't* have a drinking man."

"But, papa, *I* mean to take care of that. I've written out the temperance pledge, and dated it, and got John to sign it, and *here it is*," and she handed the paper to her father, who read it carefully, and sat turning it in his hands while his daughter went on:

"You ought to have seen how poor, how very poor they were. His wife is such a nice, quiet, hardworking woman, and has two such pretty children. I went to see them and carry them Christmas things yesterday, but it's no good doing anything if John can't get work. She told me how the poor fellow had been walking the streets in the cold, day after day, trying everywhere, and nobody would take him. It's a dreadful time now for a man to be out of work, and it isn't fair his poor wife and children should suffer. Do try him again, papa!"

"John always did better with the pineapples than anybody we have tried," said Mrs. De Witt at this point. "He is the only one who really understands pineapples."

At this moment the door opened, and there was a sound of chirping voices in the hall. "Please, Miss Florence," said Betty, "the little folks says they wants to give you a Christmas." She added in a whisper: "They thinks much of giving you something, poor little things--plaze take it of 'em." And little Tottie at the word marched in and offered the young princess his dear, beautiful, beloved string of glass beads, and Elsie presented the cross of red berries--most dear to her heart and fair to her eyes. "We wanted to give *you something*" she said bashfully.

"Oh, you lovely dears!" cried Florence; "how sweet of you! I shall keep these beautiful glass beads always, and put the cross up over my dressing-table. I thank you *ever* so much!"

"Are those John's children?" asked Mr. De Witt, winking a tear out of his eye--he was at bottom a soft-hearted old gentleman.

"Yes, papa," said Florence, caressing Elsie's curly hair,--"see how sweet they are!"

"Well--you may tell John I'll try him again." And so passed Florence's Christmas, with a new, warm sense of joy in her heart, a feeling of something in the world to be done, worth doing.

"How much joy one can give with a little money!" she said to herself as she counted over what she had spent on her Christmas. Ah yes! and how true that "It *is* more blessed to give than to receive." A shining, invisible hand was laid on her head in blessing as she lay down that night, and a sweet sense of a loving presence stole like music into her soul. Unknown to herself, she had that day taken the first step out of self-life into that life of love and care for others which brought the King of

Glory down to share earth's toils and sorrows. And that precious experience was Christ's Christmas gift to her.

DEACON PITKIN'S FARM.

CHAPTER I.
MISS DIANA.

Thanksgiving was impending in the village of Mapleton on the 20th of November, 1825.

The Governor's proclamation had been duly and truly read from the pulpit the Sunday before, to the great consternation of Miss Briskett, the ambulatory dressmaker, who declared confidentially to Deacon Pitkin's wife that "she didn't see nothin' how she was goin' to get through things--and there was Saphiry's gown, and Miss Deacon Trowbridge's cloak, and Lizy Jane's new merino, not a stroke done on't. The Governor ought to be ashamed of himself for hurrying matters so."

It was a very rash step for Miss Briskett to go to the length of such a remark about the Governor, but the deacon's wife was one of the few women who are non-conductors of indiscretion, and so the Governor never heard of it.

This particular Thanksgiving tide was marked in Mapleton by exceptionally charming weather. Once in a great while the inclement New England skies are taken with a remorseful twinge and forget to give their usual snap of September frost which generally bites off all the pretty flowers in so heart-breaking a way, and then you can have lovely times quite down through November.

It was so this year at Mapleton. Though the Thanksgiving proclamation had been read, and it was past the middle of November, yet marigolds and four-o'clocks were all ablaze in the gardens, and the golden rod and purple aster were blooming over the fields as if they were expecting to keep it up all winter.

It really is affecting, the jolly good heart with which these bright children of the rainbow flaunt and wave and dance and go on budding and blossoming in the very teeth and snarl of oncoming winter. An autumn golden rod or aster ought to be the symbol for pluck and courage, and might serve a New England crest as the broom flower did the old Plantagenets.

The trees round Mapleton were looking like gigantic tulip beds, and breaking every hour into new phantasmagoria of color; and the great elm that overshadowed the red Pitkin farm-house seemed like a dome of gold, and sent a yellow radiance through all the doors and windows as the dreamy autumn sunshine streamed through it.

The Pitkin elm was noted among the great trees of New England. Now and then Nature asserts herself and does something so astonishing and overpowering as actually to strike through the crust of human stupidity, and convince mankind that a tree is something greater than they are. As a general thing the human race has a stupid hatred of trees. They embrace every chance to cut them down. They have no idea of their fitness for anything but firewood or fruit bearing. But a great cathedral elm, with shadowy aisles of boughs, its choir of whispering winds and chanting birds, its hush and solemnity and majestic grandeur, actually conquers the dull human race and asserts its leave to be in a manner to which all hearts respond; and so the great elms of New England have got to be regarded with a sort of pride as among her very few crown jewels, and the Pitkin elm was one of these.

But wasn't it a busy time in Mapleton! Busy is no word for it. Oh, the choppings, the poundings, the stoning of raisins, the projections of pies and puddings, the killing of turkeys--who can utter it? The very chip squirrels in the stone-walls, who have a family custom of making a market-basket of their mouths, were rushing about with chops incredibly distended, and their tails had an extra whisk of thanksgiving alertness. A squirrel's Thanksgiving dinner is an affair of moment, mind you.

In the great roomy, clean kitchen of the deacon's house might be seen the lithe, comely form of Diana Pitkin presiding over the roaring great oven which was to engulf the armies of pies and cakes which were in due course of preparation on the ample tables.

Of course you want to know who Diana Pitkin was. It was a general fact about this young lady that anybody who gave one look at her, whether at church or at home, always inquired at once with effusion, "Who is she?"-- particularly if the inquirer was one of the masculine gender.

This was to be accounted for by the fact that Miss Diana presented to the first view of the gazer a dazzling combination of pink and white, a flashing pair of black eyes, a ripple of dimples about the prettiest little rosy mouth in the world, and a frequent somewhat saucy laugh, which showed a set of teeth like pearls. Add to this a quick wit, a generous though spicy temper, and a nimble tongue, and you will not wonder that Miss Diana was a marked character at Mapleton, and that the inquiry who she was was one of the most interesting facts of statistical information.

Well, she was Deacon Pitkin's second cousin, and of course just in that convenient relationship to the Pitkin boys which has all the advantages of cousinship and none of the disadvantages as may be plain to an ordinary observer. For if Miss Diana wished to ride or row or dance with any of the Pitkin boys, why shouldn't she? Were they not her cousins? But if any of these aforenamed young fellows advanced on the strength of these intimacies a presumptive claim to nearer relationship, why, then Diana was astonished--of course she had regarded them as her cousins! and she was sure she couldn't think what they could be dreaming of--"A cousin is just like a brother, you know."

This was just what James Pitkin did not believe in, and now as he is walking over hill and dale from Cambridge College to his father's house he is gathering up a decided resolution to tell Diana that he is not and will not be to her as a brother--that she must be to him all or nothing. James is the brightest, the tallest, and, the Mapleton girls said, the handsomest of the Pitkin boys. He is a strong-hearted, generous, resolute fellow as ever undertook to walk thirty-five miles home to eat his Thanksgiving dinner.

We are not sure that Miss Diana is not thinking of him quite as much as he of her, as she stands there with the long kitchen shovel in one hand, and one plump white arm thrust into the oven, and her little head cocked on one side, her brows bent, and her rosy mouth pursed up with a solemn sense of the importance of her judgment as she is testing the heat of her oven.

Oh, Di, Di! for all you seem to have nothing on your mind but the responsibility for all those pumpkin pies and cranberry tarts, we wouldn't venture a very large wager that you are not thinking about cousin James under it all at this very minute, and that all this pretty bustling housewifeliness owes its spice and flavor to the thought that James is coming to the Thanksgiving dinner.

To be sure if any one had told Di so, she would have flouted the very idea. Besides, she had privately informed Almira Sisson, her special particular confidante, that she knew Jim would come home from college full of conceit, and thinking that everybody must bow down to him, and for her part she meant to make him know his place. Of course Jim and she were good friends, etc., etc.

Oh, Di, Di! you silly, naughty girl, was it for this that you stood so long at your looking-glass last night, arranging how you would do your hair for the Thanksgiving night dance? Those killing bows which you deliberately fabricated and lodged like bright butterflies among the dark waves of your hair--who were you thinking of as you made and posed them? Lay your hand on your heart and say who to you has ever seemed the best, the truest, the bravest and kindest of your friends. But Di doesn't trouble herself with such thoughts--she only cuts out saucy mottoes from the flaky white paste to lay on the red cranberry tarts, of which she makes a special one for each cousin. For there is Bill, the second eldest, who stays at home and helps work the farm. She knows that Bill worships her very shoe-tie, and obeys all her mandates with the faithful docility of a good Newfoundland dog, and Di says "she thinks everything of Bill--she likes Bill." So she does Ed, who comes a year or two behind Bill, and is trembling out of bashful boyhood. So she does Rob and Ike and Pete and the whole healthy, ramping train who fill the Pitkin farm- house with a racket of boots and boys. So she has made every one a tart with his initial on it and a saucy motto or two, "just to keep them from being conceited, you know."

All day she keeps busy by the side of the deacon's wife--a delicate, thin, quiet little woman, with great thoughtful eyes and a step like a snowflake. New England had of old times, and has still, perhaps, in her farm-houses, these women who seem from year to year to develop in the spiritual sphere as the bodily form shrinks and fades. While the cheek grows thin and the form spare, the will-power grows daily stronger; though the outer man perish, the inner man is renewed day by day. The worn hand that seems so weak yet holds every thread and controls every movement of the most complex family life, and wonders are daily accomplished by the presence of a woman who seems little more than a spirit. The New England wife-mother was the one little jeweled pivot on which all the wheel work of the family moved.

"Well, haven't we done a good day's work, cousin?" says Diana, when ninety pies of every ilk--quince, apple, cranberry, pumpkin, and mince-- have been all safely delivered from the oven and carried up into the great vacant chamber, where, ranged in rows and frozen solid, they are to last over New Year's day! She adds, demonstratively clasping the little woman round the neck and leaning her bright cheek against her whitening hair, "Haven't we been smart?" And the calm, thoughtful eyes turn lovingly upon her as Mary Pitkin puts her arm round her and answers:

"Yes, my daughter, you have done wonderfully. We couldn't do without you!"

And Diana lifts her head and laughs. She likes petting and praising as a cat likes being stroked; but, for all that, the little puss has her claws and a sly notion of using them.

CHAPTER II.
BIAH CARTER.

It was in the flush and glow of a gorgeous sunset that you might have seen the dark form of the Pitkin farm-house rising on a green hill against the orange sky.

The red house, with its overhanging canopy of elm, stood out like an old missal picture done on a gold ground.

Through the glimmer of the yellow twilight might be seen the stacks of dry corn-stalks and heaps of golden pumpkins in the neighboring fields, from which the slow oxen were bringing home a cart well laden with farm produce.

It was the hour before supper time, and Biah Carter, the deacon's hired man, was leaning against a fence, waiting for his evening meal; indulging the while in a stream of conversational wisdom which seemed to flow all the more freely from having been dammed up through the labors of the day.

Biah was, in those far distant times of simplicity a "mute inglorious" newspaper man. Newspapers in those days were as rare and unheard of as steam cars or the telegraph, but Biah had within him all the making of a thriving modern reporter, and no paper to use it on. He was a walking biographical and statistical dictionary of all the affairs of the good folks of Mapleton. He knew every piece of furniture in their houses, and what they gave for it; every foot of land, and what it was worth; every ox, ass and sheep; every man, woman and child in town. And Biah could give pretty shrewd character pictures also, and whoever wanted to inform himself of the status of any person or thing in Mapleton would have done well to have turned the faucet of Biah's stream of talk, and watched it respectfully as it came, for it was commonly conceded that what Biah Carter didn't know about Mapleton was hardly worth knowing.

"Putty piece o' property, this 'ere farm," he said, surveying the scene around him with the air of a connoisseur. "None o' yer stun pastur land where the sheep can't get their noses down through the rocks without a file to sharpen 'em! Deacon Pitkin did a putty fair stroke o' business when he swapped off his old place for this 'ere. That are old place was all swamp land and stun pastur; wa'n't good for raisin' nothin' but juniper bushes and bull frogs. But I tell *yeu*" preceded Biah, with a shrewd wink, "that are mortgage pinches the deacon; works him like a dose of aloes and picry, it does. Deacon fairly gets lean on't."

"Why," said Abner Jenks, a stolid plow boy to whom this stream of remark was addressed; "this 'ere place ain't mortgaged, is it? Du tell, naow!"

"Why, yis; don't ye know that are? Why there's risin' two thousand dollars due on this 'ere farm, and if the deacon don't scratch for it and pay up squar to the minit, old Squire Norcross'll foreclose on him. Old squire hain't no bowels, I tell yeu, and the deacon knows he hain't: and I tell you it keeps the deacon dancin' lively as corn on a hot shovel."

"The deacon's a master hand to work," said Abner; "so's the boys."

"Wai, yis, the deacon is," said Biah, turning contemplatively to the farmhouse; "there ain't a crittur in that are house that there ain't the most work got out of 'em that ken be, down to Jed and Sam, the little uns. They work like tigers, every soul of 'em, from four o'clock in she morning' as long as they can see, and Mis' Pitkin she works all the evening--woman's work ain't never done, they say."

"She's a good woman, Mis' Pitkin is," said Abner, "and she's a smart worker."

In this phrase Abner solemnly expressed his highest ideal of a human being.

"Smart ain't no word for 't," said Biah, with alertness. "Declar for 't, the grit o' that are woman beats me. Had eight children right along in a string 'thout stoppin', done all her own work, never kep' no gal nor nothin'; allers up and dressed; allers to meetin' Sunday, and to the prayer-meetin' weekly, and never stops workin': when 'tan't one thing it's another--cookin', washin', ironin', making butter and cheese, and 'tween spells cuttin' and sewin', and if she ain't doin' that, why, she's braidin' straw to sell to the store or knitting--she's the perpetual motion ready found, Mis' Pitkin is."

"Want ter know," said the auditor, as a sort of musical rest in this monotone of talk. "Ain't she smart, though!"

"Smart! Well, I should think she was. She's over and into everything that's goin' on in that house. The deacon wouldn't know himself without her; nor wouldn't none of them boys, they just live out of her; she kind o' keeps 'em all up."

"Wal, she ain't a hefty woman, naow," said the interlocutor, who seemed to be possessed by a dim idea that worth must be weighed by the pound.

"Law bless you, no! She's a little crittur; nothin' to look to, but every bit in her is *live*. She looks pale, kind o' slips round still like moonshine, but where anything's to be done, there Mis' Pitkin is; and her hand allers goes to the right spot, and things is done afore ye know it. That are woman's kind o' still; she'll slip off and be gone to heaven some day afore folks know it. There comes the deacon and Jim over the hill. Jim walked home from college day 'fore yesterday, and turned right in to-day to help get in the taters, workin' right along. Deacon was awful grouty."

"What was the matter o' the deacon?"

"Oh, the mortgage kind o' works him. The time to pay comes round putty soon, and the deacon's face allers goes down long as yer arm. 'Tis a putty tight pull havin' Jim in college, losin' his work and havin' term bills and things to pay. Them are college folks charges *up*, I tell you. I seen it works the deacon, I heard him a-jawin' Jim 'bout it."

"What made Jim go to college?" said Abner with slow wonder in his heavy face.

"Oh, he allers was sot on eddication, and Mis' Pitkin she's sot on't, too, in her softly way, and softly women is them that giner'lly carries their p'ints, fust or last.

"But *there's* one that *ain't* softly!" Biah suddenly continued, as the vision of a black-haired, bright-eyed girl suddenly stepped forth from the doorway, and stood shading her face with her hands, looking towards the sunset. The evening light lit up a jaunty spray of golden rod that she had wreathed in her wavy hair, and gave a glow to the rounded outlines of her handsome form. "There's a sparkler for you!

And no saint, neither!" was Biah's comment. "That crittur has got more prances and capers in her than any three-year-old filly I knows on. He'll be cunning that ever gets a bridle on her."

"Some says she's going to hev Jim Pitkin, and some says it's Bill," said Abner, delighted to be able to add his mite of gossip to the stream while it was flowing.

"She's sweet on Jim while he's round, and she's sweet on Bill when Jim's up to college, and between um she gets took round to everything that going. She gives one a word over one shoulder, and one over t'other, and if the Lord above knows what's in that gal's mind or what she's up to, he knows more than I do, or she either, else I lose my bet."

Biah made this admission with a firmness that might have been a model to theologians or philosophers in general. There was a point, it appeared, where he was not omniscient. His universal statistical knowledge had a limit.

CHAPTER III.
THE SHADOW.

There is no moment of life, however festive, that does not involve the near presence of a possible tragedy. When the concert of life is playing the gayest and airiest music, it requires only the change of a little flat or sharp to modulate into the minor key.

There seemed at first glance only the elements of joyousness and gayety in the surroundings at the Pitkin farm. Thanksgiving was come--the family, healthy, rosy, and noisy, were all under the one roof-tree. There was energy, youth, intelligence, beauty, a pair of lovers on the eve of betrothal--just in that misty, golden twilight that precedes the full sunrise of avowed and accepted love--and yet behind it all was walking with stealthy step the shadow of a coming sorrow.

"What in the world ails James?" said Diana as she retreated from the door and surveyed him at a distance from her chamber window. His face was like a landscape over which a thunder-cloud has drifted, and he walked beside his father with a peculiar air of proud displeasure and repression.

At that moment the young man was struggling with the bitterest sorrow that can befall youth--the breaking up of his life-purpose. He had just come to a decision to sacrifice his hopes of education, his man's ambition, his love, his home and family, and become a wanderer on the face of the earth. How this befell requires a sketch of character.

Deacon Silas Pitkin was a fair specimen of a class of men not uncommon in New England--men too sensitive for the severe physical conditions of New England life, and therefore both suffering and inflicting suffering. He was a man of the finest moral traits, of incorruptible probity, of scrupulous honor, of an exacting conscientiousness, and of a sincere piety. But he had begun life with nothing; his whole standing in the world had been gained inch by inch by the most unremitting economy and self-denial, and he was a man of little capacity for hope, of whom it was said, in popular phraseology, that he "took things hard." He was never sanguine of good, always expectant of evil, and seemed to view life like a sentinel forbidden to sleep and constantly under arms.

For such a man to be harassed by a mortgage upon his homestead was a steady wear and drain upon his vitality. There were times when a positive horror of darkness came down upon him--when his wife's untroubled, patient hopefulness seemed to him like recklessness, when the smallest item of expense was an intolerable burden, and the very daily bread of life was full of bitterness; and when these paroxysms were upon him, one of the heaviest of his burdens was the support of his son in college. It was true that he was proud of his son's talents and sympathized with his love for learning--he had to the full that sense of the value of education which is the very vital force of the New England mind--and in an hour when things looked brighter to him he had given his consent to the scheme of a college education freely.

James was industrious, frugal, energetic, and had engaged to pay the most of his own expenses by teaching in the long winter vacations. But unfortunately this year the Mapleton Academy, which had been promised to him for the winter term, had been taken away by a little maneuver of local politics and given to another, thus leaving him without resource. This disappointment, coming just at the time when the yearly interest upon the mortgage was due, had brought upon his father one of those paroxysms of helpless gloom and discouragement in which the very world itself seemed clothed in sack-cloth.

From the time that he heard the Academy was gone, Deacon Silas lay awake nights in the blackness of darkness. "We shall all go to the poorhouse together-- that's where it will end," he said, as he tossed restlessly in the dark.

"Oh no, no, my dear," said his wife, with those serene eyes that had looked through so many gloomy hours; "we must cast our care on God."

"It's easy for women to talk. You don't have the interest money to pay, you are perfectly reckless of expense. Nothing would do but James must go to college, and now see what it's bringing us to!"

"Why, father, I thought you yourself were in favor of it."

"Well, I did wrong then. You persuaded me into it. I'd no business to have listened to you and Jim and got all this load on my shoulders."

Yet Mary Pitkin knew in her own calm, clear head that she had not been reckless of expense. The yearly interest money was ever before her, and her own incessant toils had wrought no small portion of what was needed to pay it. Her butter at the store commanded the very highest price, her straw braiding sold for a little more than that of any other hand, and she had calculated all the returns so exactly that she felt sure that the interest money for that year was safe. She had seen her husband pass through this nervous crisis many times before, and she had learned to be blamed in silence, for she was a woman out of whom all selfness had long since died, leaving only the tender pity of the nurse and the consoler. Her soul rested on her Saviour, the one ever-present, inseparable friend; and when it did no good to speak to her husband, she spoke to her God for him, and so was peaceful and peace-giving.

Even her husband himself felt her strengthening, rest-giving power, and for this reason he bore down on her with the burden of all his tremors and his cares; for while he disputed, he yet believed her, and rested upon her with an utter helpless trust, as the good angel of his house. Had *she* for a moment given way to apprehension, had *her* step been a thought less firm, her eye less peaceful, then indeed the world itself would have seemed to be sinking under his feet. Meanwhile she was to him that kind of relief which we derive from a person to whom we may say everything without a fear of its harming them. He felt quite sure that, say what he would, Mary would always be hopeful and courageous; and he felt some secret idea that his own gloomy forebodings were of service in restricting and sobering what seemed to him her too sanguine nature. He blindly reverenced, without ability fully to comprehend, her exalted religious fervor and the quietude of soul that it brought. But he did not know through how many silent conflicts, how many prayers, how many tears, how many hopes resigned and sorrows welcomed, she had come into that last refuge of sorrowful souls, that immovable peace when all life's anguish ceases and the will of God becomes the final rest.

But, unhappily for this present crisis, there was, as there often is in family life, just enough of the father's nature in the son to bring them into collision with each other. James had the same nervously anxious nature, the same intense feeling of responsibility, the same tendency towards morbid earnestness; and on that day there had come collision.

His father had poured forth upon him his fears and apprehensions in a manner which implied a censure on his son, as being willing to accept a life of scholarly ease while his father and mother were, as he expressed it, "working their lives away."

"But I tell you, father, as God is my witness, I *mean* to pay all; you shall not suffer; interest and principal--all that my work would bring--I engage to pay back."

"You!--you'll never have anything! You'll be a poor man as long as you live. Lost the Academy this Fall--that tells the story!"

"But, father, it wasn't my fault that I lost the Academy."

"It's no matter whose fault it was--that's neither here nor there--you lost it, and here you are with the vacation before you and nothing to do! There's your mother, she's working herself to death; she never gets any rest. I expect she'll go off in a consumption one of these days."

"There, there, father! that's enough! Please don't say any more. You'll see I *will* find something to do!"

There are words spoken at times in life that do not sound bitter though they come from a pitiable depth of anguish, and as James turned from his father he had taken a resolution that convulsed him with pain; his strong arms quivered with the repressed agony, and he hastily sought a distant part of the field, and began cutting and stacking corn-stalks with a nervous energy.

"Why, ye work like thunder!" was Biah's comment. "Book l'arnin' hain't spiled ye yet; your arms are good for suthin'."

"Yes, my arms are good for something, and I'll use them for something," said

Jim.

There was raging a tempest in his soul. For a young fellow of a Puritan education in those days to be angry with his father was somewhat that seemed to him as awful a sacrilege as to be angry with his God, and yet he felt that his father had been bitterly, cruelly unjust towards him. He had driven economy to the most stringent extremes; he had avoided the intimacy of his class fellows, lest he should be drawn into needless expenses; he had borne with shabby clothing and mean fare among better dressed and richer associates, and been willing to bear it. He had studied faithfully, unremittingly, for two years, but at the moment he turned from his father the throb that wrung his heart was the giving up of all. He had in his pocket a letter from his townsman and schoolmate, Sam Allen, mate of an East Indiaman just fitting out at Salem, and it said:

"We are going to sail with a picked crew, and we want one just such a fellow as you for third mate. Come along, and you can go right up, and your college mathematics will be all the better for us. Come right off, and your berth will be ready, and away for round the world!"

Here, to be sure, was immediate position--wages--employment--freedom from the intolerable burden of dependence; but it was accepted at the sacrifice of all his life's hopes. True, that in those days the experiment of a sea-faring life had often, even in instances which he recalled, brought forth fortune and an ability to settle down in peaceful competence in after life. But there was Diana. Would she wait for him? Encircled on all sides with lovers, would she keep faith with an adventurer gone for an indefinite quest? The desponding, self-distrusting side of his nature said, "No. Why should she?" Then, to go was to give up Diana--to make up his mind to have her belong to some other. Then there was his mother. An unutterable reverential pathos always to him encircled the idea of his mother. Her life to him seemed a hard one. From the outside, as he viewed it, it was all self-sacrifice and renunciation. Yet he knew that she had set her heart on an education for him, as much as it could be set on anything earthly. He was her pride, her hope; and just now that very thought was full of bitterness. There was no help for it; he must not let her work herself to death for him; he would make the household vessel lighter by the throwing himself into the sea, to sink or swim as might happen; and then, perhaps, he might come back with money to help them all.

All this was what was surging and boiling in his mind when he came in from his work to the supper that night.

CHAPTER IV.
THE GOOD-BY.

Diana Pitkin was like some of the fruits of her native hills, full of juices which tend to sweetness in maturity, but which when not quite ripe have a pretty decided dash of sharpness. There are grapes that require a frost to ripen them, and Diana was somewhat akin to these.

She was a mettlesome, warm-blooded creature, full of the energy and audacity of youth, to whom as yet life was only a frolic and a play spell. Work never tired her. She ate heartily, slept peacefully, went to bed laughing, and got up in a merry humor in the morning. Diana's laugh was as early a note as the song of birds. Such a nature is not at first sympathetic. It has in it some of the unconscious cruelty which belongs to nature itself, whose sunshine never pales at human trouble. Eyes that have never wept cannot comprehend sorrow. Moreover, a lively girl of eighteen, looking at life out of eyes which bewilder others with their brightness, does not always see the world truly, and is sometimes judged to be heartless when she is only immature.

Nothing was further from Diana's thoughts than that any grave trouble was overhanging her lover's mind--for her lover she very well knew that James was, and she had arranged beforehand to herself very pretty little comedies of life, to be duly enacted in the long vacation, in which James was to appear as the suitor, and she, not too soon nor with too much eagerness, was at last to acknowledge to him how much he was to her. But meanwhile he was not to be too presumptuous. It was not set down in the cards that she should be too gracious or make his way too easy. When, therefore, he brushed by her hastily, on entering the house, with a flushed cheek and frowning brow, and gave no glance of admiration at the pretty toilet she had found time to make, she was slightly indignant. She was as ignorant of the pang which went like an arrow through his heart at the sight of her as the bobolink which whirrs and chitters and tweedles over a grave.

She turned away and commenced a kitten-like frolic with Bill, who was always only too happy to second any of her motions, and readily promised that after supper she would go with him a walk of half a mile over to a neighbor's, where was a corn-husking. A great golden lamp of a harvest moon was already coming up in the fading flush of the evening sky, and she promised herself much amusement in watching the result of her maneuver on James.

"He'll see at any rate that I am not waiting his beck and call. Next time, if he wants my company he can ask for it in season. I'm not going to indulge him in sulks, not I. These college fellows worry over books till they hurt their digestion, and then have the blues and look as if the world was coming to an end." And Diana went to the looking-glass and rearranged the spray of golden-rod in her hair and nodded at herself defiantly, and then turned to help get on the supper.

The Pitkin folk that night sat down to an ample feast, over which the impending Thanksgiving shed its hilarity. There was not only the inevitable great pewter platter, scoured to silver brightness, in the center of the table, and piled with solid masses of boiled beef, pork, cabbage and all sorts of vegetables, and the equally inevitable smoking loaf of rye and Indian bread, to accompany the pot of baked pork and beans, but there were specimens of all the newly-made Thanksgiving pies filling every available space on the table. Diana set special value on herself as a pie artist, and she had taxed her ingenuity this year to invent new varieties, which were received with bursts of applause by the boys. These sat down to the table in democratic equality,--Biah Carter and Abner with all the sons of the family, old and young, each eager, hungry and noisy; and over all, with moonlight calmness and steadiness, Mary Pitkin ruled and presided, dispensing to each his portion in due season, while Diana, restless and mischievous as a sprite, seemed to be possessed with an elfin spirit of drollery, venting itself in sundry little tricks and antics which drew ready laughs from the boys and reproving glances from the deacon. For the deacon was that night in one of his severest humors. As Biah Carter afterwards remarked of that night, "You could feel there was thunder in the air somewhere round. The deacon had got on about his longest face, and when the deacon's face is about down to its wust, why, it would stop a robin singin'--there couldn't nothin' stan' it."

To-night the severely cut lines of his face had even more than usual of haggard sternness, and the handsome features of James beside him, in their fixed gravity, presented that singular likeness which often comes out between father and son in seasons of mental emotion. Diana in vain sought to draw a laugh from her cousin. In pouring his home-brewed beer she contrived to spatter him, but he wiped it off without a smile, and let pass in silence some arrows of raillery that she had directed at his somber face.

When they rose from table, however, he followed her into the pantry.

"Diana, will you take a walk with me to-night?" he said, in a voice husky with repressed feeling.

"To-night! Why, I have just promised Bill to go with him over to the husking at the Jenks's. Why don't you go with us? We're going to have lots of fun," she added with an innocent air of not perceiving his gravity.

"I can't," he said. "Besides I wanted to walk with you alone. I had something special I wanted to say."

"Bless me, how you frighten one! You look solemn as a hearse; but I promised to go with Bill to-night, and I suspect another time will do just as well. What you have to say will *keep*, I suppose," she said mischievously.

He turned away quickly.

"I should really like to know what's the matter with you to-night," she added, but as she spoke he went up-stairs and shut the door.

"He's cross to-night," was Diana's comment. "Well, he'll have to get over his pet. I sha'n't mind it!"

Up-stairs in his room James began the work of putting up the bundle with which he was to go forth to seek his fortune. There stood his books, silent and dear witnesses of the world of hope and culture and refined enjoyment he had been meaning to enter. He was to know them no more. Their mute faces seemed to look at him mournfully as parting friends. He rapidly made his selection, for that night he was to be off in time to reach the vessel before she sailed, and he felt even glad to avoid the Thanksgiving festivities for which he had so little relish. Diana's frolicsome gaiety seemed heart-breaking to him, on the same principle that the poet sings:

"How can ye chant, ye little birds, And I sae weary, fu' o' care?"

To the heart struck through with its first experiences of real suffering all nature is full of cruelty, and the young and light-hearted are a large part of nature.

"She has no feeling," he said to himself. "Well, there is one reason the more for my going. *She* won't break her heart for me; nobody loves me but mother, and it's for her sake I must go. She mustn't work herself to death for me."

And then he sat down in the window to write a note to be given to his mother after he had sailed, for he could not trust himself to tell her what he was about to do. He knew that she would try to persuade him to stay, and he felt faint-hearted when he thought of her. "She would sit up early and late, and work for me to the last gasp," he thought, "but father was right. It is selfish of me to take it," and so he sat trying to fashion his parting note into a tone of cheerfulness.

"My dear mother," he wrote, "this will come to you when I have set off on a four years' voyage round the world. Father has convinced me that it's time for me to be doing something for myself; and I couldn't get a school to keep--and, after all, education is got other ways than at college. It's hard to go, because I love home, and hard because you will miss me-- though no one else will. But father may rely upon it, I will not be a burden on him another day. Sink or swim, I shall *never* come back till I have enough to do for myself, and you too. So good bye, dear mother. I know you will always pray for me, and wherever I am I shall try to do just as I think you would want me to do. I know your prayers will follow me, and I shall always be your affectionate son.

"P.S.--The boys may have those chestnuts and walnuts in my room--and in my drawer there is a bit of ribbon with a locket on it I was going to give cousin Diana. Perhaps she won't care for it, though; but if she does, she is welcome to it--it may put her in mind of old times."'

And this is all he said, with bitterness in his heart, as he leaned on the window and looked out at the great yellow moon that was shining so bright as to show the golden hues of the overhanging elm boughs and the scarlet of an adjoining maple.

A light ripple of laughter came up from below, and a chestnut thrown up struck him on the hand, and he saw Diana and Bill step from out the shadowy porch.

"There's a chestnut for you, Mr. Owl," she called, gaily, "if you *will* stay moping up there! Come, now, it's a splendid evening; *won't* you come?"

"No, thank you. I sha'n't be missed," was the reply.

"That's true enough; the loss is your own. Good bye, Mr. Philosopher."

"Good bye, Diana."

Something in the tone struck strangely through her heart. It was the voice of what Diana never had felt yet--deep suffering--and she gave a little shiver.

"What an *awfully* solemn voice James has sometimes," she said; and then added, with a laugh, "it would make his fortune as a Methodist minister."

The sound of the light laugh and little snatches and echoes of gay talk came back like heartless elves to mock Jim's sorrow.

"So much for *her*," he said, and turned to go and look for his mother.

CHAPTER V.
MOTHER AND SON.

He knew where he should find her. There was a little, low work-room adjoining the kitchen that was his mother's sanctum. There stood her work-basket--there were always piles and piles of work, begun or finished; and there also her few books at hand, to be glanced into in rare snatches of leisure in her busy life.

The old times New England house mother was not a mere unreflective drudge of domestic toil. She was a reader and a thinker, keenly appreciative in intellectual regions. The literature of that day in New England was sparse; but whatever there was, whether in this country or in England, that was noteworthy, was matter of keen interest, and Mrs. Pitkin's small library was very dear to her. No nun in a convent under vows of abstinence ever practiced more rigorous self-denial than she did in the restraints and government of intellectual tastes and desires. Her son was dear to her as the fulfillment and expression of her unsatisfied craving for knowledge, the possessor of those fair fields of thought which duty forbade her to explore.

James stood and looked in at the window, and saw her sorting and arranging the family mending, busy over piles of stockings and shirts, while on the table beside her lay her open Bible, and she was singing to herself, in a low, sweet undertone, one of the favorite minor-keyed melodies of those days:

"O God, our help in ages past,   Our hope for years to come, Our shelter from the stormy blast   And our eternal home!"

An indescribable feeling, blended of pity and reverence, swelled in his heart as he looked at her and marked the whitening hair, the thin worn little hands so busy with their love work, and thought of all the bearing and forbearing, the waiting, the watching, the long-suffering that had made up her life for so many years. The very look of exquisite calm and resolved strength in her patient eyes and in the gentle lines of her face had something that seemed to him sad and awful--as the purely spiritual always looks to the more animal nature. With his blood bounding and tingling in his veins, his strong arms pulsating with life, and his heart full of a man's vigor and resolve, his mother's life seemed to him to be one of weariness and drudgery, of constant, unceasing self-abnegation. Calm he knew she was, always sustained, never faltering; but her victory was one which, like the spiritual sweetness in the face of the dying, had something of sadness for the living heart.

He opened the door and came in, sat down by her on the floor, and laid his head in her lap.

"Mother, you never rest; you never stop working."

"Oh, no!" she said gaily, "I'm just going to stop now. I had only a few last things I wanted to get done."

"Mother, I can't bear to think of you; your life is too hard. We all have our amusements, our rests, our changes; your work is never done; you are worn out, and get no time to read, no time for anything but drudgery."

"Don't say drudgery, my boy--work done for those we love **never** is drudgery. I'm so happy to have you all around me I never feel it."

"But, mother, you are not strong, and I don't see how you can hold out to do all you do."

"Well," she said simply, "when my strength is all gone I ask God for more, and he always gives it. 'They that wait on the Lord shall renew their strength.'" And her hand involuntarily fell on the open Bible.

"Yes, I know it," he said, following her hand with his eyes--while "Mother," he said, "I want you to give me your Bible and take mine. I think yours would do me more good."

There was a little bright flush and a pleased smile on his mother's face--

"Certainly, my boy, I will."

"I see you have marked your favorite places," he added. "It will seem like hearing you speak to read them."

"With all my heart," she added, taking up the Bible and kissing his forehead as she put it into his hands.

There was a struggle in his heart how to say farewell without saying it-- without letting her know that he was going to leave her. He clasped her in his arms and kissed her again and again.

"Mother," he said, "if I ever get into heaven it will be through you."

"Don't say that, my son--it must be through a better Friend than I am-- who loves you more than I do. I have not died for you--He did."

"Oh, that I knew where I might find him, then. You I can see--Him I cannot."

His mother looked at him with a face full of radiance, pity, and hope.

"I feel sure you *will*" she said. "You are consecrated," she added, in a low voice, laying her hand on his head.

"Amen," said James, in a reverential tone. He felt that she was at that moment--as she often was--silently speaking to One invisible of and for him, and the sense of it stole over him like a benediction. There was a pause of tender silence for many minutes.

"Well, I must not keep you up any longer, mother dear--it's time you were resting. Good-night." And with a long embrace and kiss they separated. He had yet fifteen miles to walk to reach the midnight stage that was to convey him to Salem.

As he was starting from the house with his bundle in his hand, the sound of a gay laugh came through the distant shrubbery. It was Diana and Bill returning from the husking. Hastily he concealed himself behind a clump of old lilac bushes till they emerged into the moonlight and passed into the house. Diana was in one of those paroxysms of young girl frolic which are the effervescence of young, healthy blood, as natural as the gyrations of a bobolink on a clover head. James was thinking of dark nights and stormy seas, years of exile, mother's sorrows, home perhaps never to be seen more, and the laugh jarred on him like a terrible discord. He watched her into the house, turned, and was gone.

CHAPTER VI.
GONE TO SEA.

A little way on in his moonlight walk James's ears were saluted by the sound of some one whistling and crackling through the bushes, and soon Biah Carter, emerged into the moonlight, having been out to the same husking where Diana and Bill had been enjoying themselves. The sight of him resolved a doubt which had been agitating James's mind. The note to his mother which was to explain his absence and the reasons for it was still in his coat-pocket, and he had designed sending it back by some messenger at the tavern where he took the midnight stage; but here was a more trusty party. It involved, to be sure, the necessity of taking Biah into his confidence. James was well aware that to tell that acute individual the least particle of a story was like starting a gimlet in a pine board--there was no stop till it had gone through. So he told him in brief that a good berth had been offered to him on the **Eastern Star**, and he meant to take it to relieve his father of the pressure of his education.

"Wal naow--you don't say so," was Biah's commentary. "Wal, yis, 'tis hard sleddin' for the deacon--drefful hard sleddin.' Wal, naow, s'pose you're disapp'inted--shouldn't wonder--jes' so. Eddication's a good thing, but 'taint the only thing naow; folks larns a sight rubbin' round the world-- and then they make money. Jes' see, there's Cap'n Stebbins and Cap'n Andrews and Cap'n Merryweather--all livin' on good farms, with good, nice houses, all got goin' to sea. Expect Mis' Pitkin'll take it sort o' hard, she's so sot on you; but she's allers sayin' things is for the best, and maybe she'll come to think so 'bout this--folks gen'ally does when they can't help themselves. Wal, yis, naow--goin' to walk to the cross-road tavern? better not. Jest wait a minit and I'll hitch up and take ye over.

"Thank you, Biah, but I can't stop, and I'd rather walk, so I won't trouble you."

"Wal, look here--don't ye want a sort o' nest-egg? I've got fifty silver dollars laid up: you take it on venture and give me half what it brings."

"Thank you, Biah. If you'll trust me with it I'll hope to do something for us both."

Biah went into the house, and after some fumbling brought out a canvas bag, which he put into James's hand.

"Wanted to go to sea confoundedly myself, but there's Mariar Jane--she won't hear on't, and turns on the water-works if I peep a single word. Farmin's dreffful slow, but when a feller's got a gal he's got a cap'n; he has to mind orders. So you jest trade and we'll go sheers. I think consid'able of you, and I expect you'll make it go as fur as anybody."

"I'll try my best, you may believe, Biah," said James, shaking the hard hand heartily, as he turned on his way towards the cross-roads tavern.

The whole village of Maplewood on Thanksgiving Day morning was possessed of the fact that James Pitkin had gone off to sea in the *Eastern Star*, for Biah had felt all the sense of importance which the possession of a startling piece of intelligence gives to one, and took occasion to call at the tavern and store on his way up and make the most of his information, so that by the time the bell rang for service the news might be said to be everywhere. The minister's general custom on Thanksgiving Day was to get off a political sermon reviewing the State of New England, the United States of America, and Europe, Asia, and Africa; but it may be doubted if all the affairs of all these continents produced as much sensation among the girls in the singers' seat that day as did the news that James Pitkin had gone to sea on a four years' voyage. Curious eyes were cast on Diana Pitkin, and many were the whispers and speculations as to the part she might have had in the move; and certainly she looked paler and graver than usual, and some thought they could detect traces of tears on her cheeks. Some noticed in the tones of her voice that day, as they rose in the soprano, a tremor and pathos never remarked before--the unconscious utterance of a new sense of sorrow, awakened in a soul that up to this time had never known a grief.

For the letter had fallen on the heads of the Pitkin household like a thunderbolt. Biah came in to breakfast and gave it to Mrs. Pitkin, saying that James had handed him that last night, on his way over to take the midnight stage to Salem, where he was going to sail on the *Eastern Star* to-day--no doubt he's off to sea by this time. A confused sound of exclamations went up around the table, while Mrs. Pitkin, pale and calm, read the letter and then passed it to her husband without a word. The bright, fixed color in Diana's face had meanwhile been slowly ebbing away, till, with cheeks and lips pale as ashes, she hastily rose and left the table and went to her room. A strange, new, terrible pain--a sensation like being choked or smothered--a rush of mixed emotions--a fearful sense of some inexorable, unalterable crisis having come of her girlish folly--overwhelmed her. Again she remembered the deep tones of his good-by, and how she had only mocked at his emotion. She sat down and leaned her head on her hands in a tearless, confused sorrow.

Deacon' Pitkin was at first more shocked and overwhelmed than his wife. His yesterday's talk with James had no such serious purpose. It had been only the escape-valve for his hypochondriac forebodings of the future, and nothing was farther from his thoughts than having it bear fruit in any such decisive movement on the part of his son. In fact, he secretly was proud of his talents and his scholarship, and had set his heart on his going through college, and had no more serious purpose in what he said the day before than the general one of making his son feel the difficulties and straits he was put to for him. Young men were tempted at college to be too expensive, he thought, and to forget what it cost their parents at home. In short, the whole thing had been merely the passing off of a paroxysm of hypochondria, and he had already begun to be satisfied that he should raise his interest money that year without material difficulty. The letter showed him too keenly the depth of the suffering he had inflicted on his son, and when he had read it he cast a sort of helpless, questioning look on his wife, and said, after an interval of silence:

"Well, mother!"

There was something quite pathetic in the appealing look and voice.'

"Well, father," she answered in subdued tones; "all we can do now is to *leave* it."

LEAVE IT!

Those were words often in that woman's mouth, and they expressed that habit of her life which made her victorious over all troubles, that habit of trust in the Infinite Will that actually could and did *leave* every accomplished event in His hand, without murmur and without conflict.

If there was any one thing in her uniformly self-denied life that had been a personal ambition and a personal desire, it had been that her son should have a college education. It was the center of her earthly wishes, hopes and efforts. That wish had been cut off in a moment, that hope had sunk under her feet, and now only remained to her the task of comforting the undisciplined soul whose unguided utterances had wrought the mischief. It was not the first time that, wounded by a loving hand in this dark struggle of life, she had suppressed the pain of her own hurt that he that had wounded her might the better forgive himself.

"Dear father," she said to him, when over and over he blamed himself for his yesterday's harsh words to his son, "don't worry about it now; you didn't mean it. James is a good boy, and he'll see it right at last; and he is in God's hands, and we must leave him there. He overrules all."

When Mrs. Pitkin turned from her husband she sought Diana in her room.

"Oh, cousin! cousin!" said the girl, throwing herself into her arms. "*Is* this true? Is James *gone*? Can't we do *any* thing? Can't we get him back? I've been thinking it over. Oh, if the ship wouldn't sail! and I'd go to Salem and beg him to come back, on my knees. Oh, if I had only known yesterday! Oh, cousin, cousin! he wanted to talk with me, and I wouldn't hear him!--oh, if I only had, I could have persuaded him out of it! Oh, why didn't I know?"

"There, there, dear child! We must accept it just as it is, now that it is done. Don't feel so. We must try to look at the good."

"Oh, show me that letter," said Diana; and Mrs. Pitkin, hoping to tranquil-ize her, gave her James's note. "He thinks I don't care for him," she said, reading it hastily. "Well, I don't wonder! But I *do* care! I love him better than anybody or anything under the sun, and I never will forget him; he's a brave, noble, good man, and I shall love him as long as I live--I don't care who knows it! Give me that locket, cousin, and write to him that I shall wear it to my grave."

"Dear child, there is no writing to him."

"Oh, dear! that's the worst. Oh, that horrid, horrid sea! It's like death--you don't know where they are, and you can't hear from them--and a four years' voy-age! Oh, dear! oh, dear!"

"Don't, dear child, don't; you distress me," said Mrs. Pitkin.

"Yes, that's just like me," said Diana, wiping her eyes. "Here I am thinking only of myself, and you that have had your heart broken are trying to comfort me, and trying to comfort Cousin Silas. We have both of us scolded and flouted him away, and now you, who suffer the most of either of us, spend your breath to comfort us. It's just like you. But, cousin, I'll try to be good and comfort you. I'll try to be a daughter to you. You need somebody to think of you, for you never think of your-self. Let's go in his room," she said, and taking the mother by the hand they crossed to the empty room. There was his writing-table, there his forsaken books, his papers, some of his clothes hanging in his closet. Mrs. Pitkin, opening a drawer, took out a locket hung upon a bit of blue ribbon, where there were two locks of hair, one of which Diana recognized as her own, and one of James's. She hastily hung it about her neck and concealed it in her bosom, laying her hand hard upon it, as if she would still the beatings of her heart.

"It seems like a death," she said. "Don't you think the ocean is like death--wide, dark, stormy, unknown? We cannot speak to or hear from them that are on it."

"But people can and do come back from the sea," said the mother, soothingly. "I trust, in God's own time, we shall see James back."

"But what if we never should? Oh, cousin! I can't help thinking of that. There was Michael Davis,--you know--the ship was never heard from."

"Well," said the mother, after a moment's pause and a choking down of some rising emotion, and turning to a table on which lay a Bible, she opened and read: "If I take the wings of the morning and dwell in the uttermost parts of the sea, even there shall Thy hand lead me, and Thy right hand shall hold me."

The THEE in this psalm was not to her a name, a shadow, a cipher, to designate the unknowable--it stood for the inseparable Heart-friend--the Father seeing in secret, on whose bosom all her tears of sorrow had been shed, the Comforter and Guide forever dwelling in her soul, and giving peace where the world gave only trouble.

Diana beheld her face as it had been the face of an angel. She kissed her, and turned away in silence.

CHAPTER VII.
THANKSGIVING AGAIN.

Seven years had passed and once more the Thanksgiving tide was in Mapleton. This year it had come cold and frosty. Chill driving autumn storms had stripped the painted glories from the trees, and remorseless frosts had chased the hardy ranks of the asters and golden-rods back and back till scarce a blossom could be found in the deepest and most sequestered spots. The great elm over the Pitkin farm-house had been stripped of its golden glory, and now rose against the yellow evening sky, with its infinite delicacies of net work and tracery, in their way quite as beautiful as the full pomp of summer foliage. The air without was keen and frosty, and the knotted twigs of the branches knocked against the roof and rattled and ticked against the upper window panes as the chill evening wind swept through them.

Seven long years had passed since James sailed. Years of watching, of waiting, of cheerful patience, at first, and at last of resigned sorrow. Once they heard from James, at the first port where the ship stopped. It was a letter dear to his mother's heart, manly, resigned and Christian; expressing full purpose to work with God in whatever calling he should labor, and cheerful hopes of the future. Then came a long, long silence, and then tidings that the **Eastern Star** had been wrecked on a reef in the Indian ocean! The mother had given back her treasure into the same beloved hands whence she first received him. "I gave him to God, and God took him," she said. "I shall have him again in God's time." This was how she settled the whole matter with herself. Diana had mourned with all the vehement intensity of her being, but out of the deep baptism of sorrow she had emerged with a new and nobler nature. The vain, trifling, laughing Undine had received a soul and was a true woman. She devoted herself to James's mother with an utter self-sacrificing devotion, resolved as far as in her lay to be both son and daughter to her. She read, and studied, and fitted herself as a teacher in a neighboring academy, and persisted in claiming the right of a daughter to place all the amount of her earnings in the family purse.

And this year there was special need. With all his care, with all his hard work and that of his family, Deacon Silas never had been able to raise money to annihilate the debt upon the farm.

There seemed to be a perfect fatality about it. Let them all make what exertions they might, just as they were hoping for a sum that should exceed the interest and begin the work of settling the principal would come some loss that would throw them all back. One year their barn was burned just as they had housed their hay. On another a valuable horse died, and then there were fits of sickness among the children, and poor crops in the field, and low prices in the market; in short, as Biah remarked, "The deacon's luck did seem to be a sort o' streaky, for do what you might there's always suthin' to put him back." As the younger boys grew up the deacon had ceased to hire help, and Biah had transferred his services to Squire Jones, a rich landholder in the neighborhood, who wanted some one to overlook his place. The increased wages had enabled him to give a home to Maria Jane and a start in life to two or three sturdy little American citizens who played around his house door. Nevertheless, Biah never lost sight of the "deacon's folks" in his multifarious cares, and never missed an opportunity either of doing them a good turn or of picking up any stray item of domestic news as to how matters were going on in that interior. He had privately broached the theory to Miss Briskett, "that arter all it was James that Diany (he always pronounced all names as if they ended in y) was sot on, and that she took it so hard, his goin' off, that it did beat all! Seemed to make another gal of her; he shouldn't wonder if she'd come out and jine the church." And Diana not long after unconsciously fulfilled Biah's predictions.

Of late Biah's good offices had been in special requisition, as the deacon had been for nearly a month on a sick bed with one of those interminable attacks of typhus fever which used to prevail in old times, when the doctor did everything he could to make it certain that a man once brought down with sickness never should rise again.

But Silas Pitkin had a constitution derived through an indefinite distance from a temperate, hard-working, godly ancestry, and so withstood both death and the doctor, and was alive and in a convalescent state, which gave hope of his being able to carve the turkey at his Thanksgiving dinner.

The evening sunlight was just fading out of the little "keeping-room," adjoining the bed-room, where the convalescent now was able to sit up most of the day. A cot bed had been placed there, designed for him to lie down upon in intervals of fatigue. At present, however, he was sitting in his arm-chair, complacently watching the blaze of the hickory fire, or following placidly the motions of his wife's knitting-needles.

There was an air of calmness and repose on his thin, worn features that never was there in days of old: the haggard, anxious lines had been smoothed away, and that spiritual expression which sickness and sorrow sometimes develops on the human face reigned in its place. It was the "clear shining after rain."

"Wife," he said, "read me something I can't quite remember out of the Bible. It's in the eighth of Deuteronomy, the second verse."

Mrs. Pitkin opened the big family Bible on the stand, and read, "And thou shalt remember all the way in which the Lord thy God hath led thee these forty years in the wilderness, to humble thee and to prove thee and to know what is in thy heart, and whether thou wouldst keep his commandments or no. And he humbled thee, and suffered thee to hunger, and fed thee with manna, which thou knewest not, neither did thy fathers know, that he might make thee know that man doth not live by bread alone, but by every word that proceedeth out of the mouth of the Lord doth man live."

"There, that's it," interrupted the deacon. "That's what I've been thinking of as I've lain here sick and helpless. I've fought hard to keep things straight and clear the farm, but it's pleased the Lord to bring me low. I've had to lie still and leave all in his hands."

"And where better could you leave all?" said his wife, with a radiant smile.

"Well, just so. I've been saying, 'Here I am, Lord; do with me as seemeth to thee good,' and I feel a great quiet now. I think it's doubtful if we make up the interest this year. I don't know what Bill may get for the hay: but I don't see much prospect of raisin' on't; and yet I don't worry. Even if it's the Lord's will to have the place sold up and we be turned out in our old age, I don't seem to worry about it. His will be done."

There was a sound of rattling wheels at this moment, and anon there came a brush and flutter of garments, and Diana rushed in, all breezy with the freshness of out-door air, and caught Mrs. Pitkin in her arms and kissed her first and then the deacon with effusion.

"Here I come for Thanksgiving," she said, in a rich, clear tone, "and here," she added, drawing a roll of bills from her bosom, and putting it into the deacon's hand, "here's the interest money for this year. I got it all myself, because I wanted to show you I could be good for something."

"Thank you, dear daughter," said Mrs. Pitkin. "I felt sure some way would be found and now I see *what*." She added, kissing Diana and patting her rosy cheek, "a very pleasant, pretty way it is, too."

"I was afraid that Uncle Silas would worry and put himself back again about the interest money," said Diana.

"Well, daughter," said the Deacon, "it's a pity we should go through all we do in this world and not learn anything by it. I hope the Lord has taught me not to worry, but just do my best and leave myself and everything else in his hands. We can't help ourselves--we can't make one hair white or black. Why should we wear our lives out fretting? If I'd a known *that* years ago it would a been better for us all."

"Never mind, father, you know it now," said his wife, with a face serene as a star. In this last gift of quietude of soul to her husband she recognized the answer to her prayers of years.

"Well now," said Diana, running to the window, "I should like to know what Biah Carter is coming here about."

"Oh, Biah's been very kind to us in this sickness," said Mrs. Pitkin, as Biah's feet resounded on the scraper.

"Good evenin', Deacon," said Biah, entering, "Good evenin', Mrs. Pitkin. Sarvant, ma'am," to Diana--"how ye all gettin' on?"

"Nicely, Biah--well as can be," said Mrs. Pitkin.

"Wal, you see I was up to the store with some o' Squire Jones's bell flowers. Sim Coan he said he wanted some to sell, and so I took up a couple o' barrels, and I see the darndest big letter there for the Deacon. Miss Briskett she was in, lookin' at it, and so was Deacon Simson's wife; she come in arter some cinnamon sticks. Wal, and they all looked at it and talked it over, and couldn't none o' 'em for their lives think what it's all about, it was sich an almighty thick letter," said Biah, drawing out a long, legal-looking envelope and putting it in the Deacon's hands.

"I hope there isn't bad news in it," said Silas Pitkin, the color flushing apprehensively in his pale cheeks as he felt for his spectacles.

There was an agitated, silent pause while he broke the seals and took out two documents. One was the mortgage on his farm and the other a receipt in full for the money owed on it! The Deacon turned the papers to and fro, gazed on them with a dazed, uncertain air and then said:

"Why, mother, do look! *Is* this so? Do I read it right?"

"Certainly, you do," said Diana, reading over his shoulder. "Somebody's paid that debt, uncle!"

"Thank God!" said Mrs. Pitkin, softly; "He has done it."

"Wal, I swow!" said Biah, after having turned the paper in his hands, "if this 'ere don't beat all! There's old Squire Norcross's name on't. It's the receipt, full and square. What's come over the old crittur? He must a' got religion in his old' age; but if grace made him do *that*, grace has done a tough job, that's all; but it's done anyhow! and that's all you need to care about. Wal, wal, I must git along hum--Mariar Jane'll be wonderin' where I be. Good night, all on ye!" and Biah's retreating wagon wheels were off in the distance, rattling furiously, for, notwithstanding Maria Jane's wondering, Biah was resolved not to let an hour slip by without declaring the wonderful tidings at the store.

The Pitkin family were seated at supper in the big kitchen, all jubilant over the recent news. The father, radiant with the pleasantest excitement, had for the first time come out to take his place at the family board. In the seven years since the beginning of our story the Pitkin boys had been growing apace, and now surrounded the table quite an army of rosy-cheeked, jolly young fellows, who to-night were in a perfect tumult of animal gaiety. Diana twinkled and dimpled and flung her sparkles round among them, and there was unbounded jollity.

"Who's that looking in at the window?" called out Sam, aged ten, who sat opposite the house door. At that moment the door opened, and a dark stranger, bronzed with travel and dressed in foreign-looking garments, entered.

He stood one moment, all looking curiously at him, then crossing the floor, he kneeled down by Mrs. Pitkin's chair, and throwing off his cap, looked her close in the eyes.

"Mother, don't you know me?"

She looked at him one moment with that still earnestness peculiar to herself, and then fell into his arms. "O my son, my son!"

There were a few moments of indescribable confusion, during which Diana retreated, pale and breathless, to a neighboring window, and stood with her hand over the locket which she had always worn upon her heart.

After a few moments he came, and she felt him by her.

"What, cousin!" he said; "no welcome from you?" She gave one look, and he took her in his arms. She felt the beating of his heart, and he felt hers. Neither spoke, yet each felt at that moment sure of the other.

"I say, boys," said James, "who'll help bring in my sea chest?"

Never was sea chest more triumphantly ushered; it was a contest who should get near enough to take some part in it's introduction, and soon it was open, and James began distributing its contents.

"There, mother," said he, undoing a heavy black India satin and shaking out its folds, "I'm determined you shall have a dress fit for you; and here's a real India shawl to go with it. Get those on and you'll look as much like a queen among women as you ought to."

Then followed something for every member of the family, received with frantic demonstrations of applause and appreciation by the more juvenile.

"Oh, what's that?" said Sam, as a package done up in silk paper and tied with silver cord was disclosed.

"That's--oh--that's my wife's wedding-dress," said James, unfolding and shaking out a rich satin; "and here's her shawl," drawing out an embroidered box, scented with sandal-wood.

The boys all looked at Diana, and Diana laughed and grew pale and red all in the same breath, as James, folding back the silk and shawl in their boxes, handed them to her.

Mrs. Pitkin laughed and kissed her, and said, gaily, "All right, my daughter--just right."

What an evening that was, to be sure! What a confusion of joy and gladness! What a half-telling of a hundred things that it would take weeks to tell.

James had paid the mortgage and had money to spare; and how he got it all, and how he was saved at sea, and where he went, and what befell him here and there, he promised to be telling them for six months to come.

"Well, your father mustn't be kept up too late," said Mrs. Pitkin. "Let's have prayers now, and then to-morrow we'll be fresh to talk more."

So they gathered around the wide kitchen fire and the family Bible was brought out.

"Father," said James, drawing out of his pocket the Bible his mother had given him at parting, "let me read my Psalm; it has been my Psalm ever since I left you." There was a solemn thrill in the little circle as James read the verses:

"They that go down to the sea in ships, that do business in great waters; these see the works of the Lord and his wonders in the deep. For he commandeth and raiseth the stormy wind which lifteth up the waves thereof. They mount up to the heaven; they go down again to the depths: their soul is melted because of trouble. Then they cry unto the Lord in their trouble, and he bringeth them out of their distresses. He maketh the storm a calm, so that the waves thereof are still. Then are they glad because they be quiet, so he bringeth them unto their desired haven. Oh that men would praise the Lord for his goodness, and for his wonderful works to the children of men!"

*   *   *   *   *

When all had left the old kitchen, James and Diana sat by the yet glowing hearth and listened to the crickets, and talked over all the past and the future.

"And now," said James, "it's seven years since I left you, and to-morrow is the seventh Thanksgiving, and I've always set my heart on getting home to be married Thanksgiving evening."

"But, dear me, Jim, we can't. There isn't time."

"Why not?--we've got all the time there is!"

"But the wedding-dress can't be made, possibly."

"Oh, that can wait till the week after. You are pretty enough without it!"

"But what will they all say?"

"Who cares what they say? I don't," said James. "The fact is, I've set my heart on it, and you owe me something for the way you treated me the last Thanksgiving I was here, seven years ago. Now don't you?"

"Well, yes, I do, so have it just as you will." And so it was accomplished the next evening.

And among the wonders of Mapleton Miss Briskett announced it as chief, that it was the first time she ever heard of a bride that was married first and had her wedding-dress made the week after! She never had heard of such a thing.

Yet, strange to say, for years after neither of the parties concerned found themselves a bit the worse for it.

THE FIRST CHRISTMAS OF NEW ENGLAND.

The shores of the Atlantic coast of America may well be a terror to navigators. They present an inexorable wall, against which forbidding and angry waves incessantly dash, and around which shifting winds continually rave. The approaches to safe harbors are few in number, intricate and difficult, requiring the skill of practiced pilots.

But, as if with a pitying spirit of hospitality, old Cape Cod, breaking from the iron line of the coast, like a generous-hearted sailor intent on helpfulness, stretches an hundred miles outward, and, curving his sheltering arms in a protective circle, gives a noble harborage. Of this harbor of Cape Cod the report of our governmental Coast Survey thus speaks: "It is one of the finest harbors for ships of war on the whole of our Atlantic coast. The width and freedom from obstruction of every kind at its entrance and the extent of sea room upon the bay side make it accessible to vessels of the largest class in almost all winds. This advantage, its capacity, depth of water, excellent anchorage, and the complete shelter it affords from all winds, render it one of the most valuable ship harbors upon our coast."

We have been thus particular in our mention of this place, because here, in this harbor, opened the first scene in the most wonderful drama of modern history.

Let us look into the magic mirror of the past and see this harbor of Cape Cod on the morning of the 11th of November, in the year of our Lord 1620, as described to us in the simple words of the pilgrims: "A pleasant bay, circled round, except the entrance, which is about four miles over from land to land, ***compassed about to the very sea*** with oaks, pines, junipers, sassafras, and other sweet weeds. It is a harbor wherein a thousand sail of ship may safely ride."

Such are the woody shores of Cape Cod as we look back upon them in that distant November day, and the harbor lies like a great crystal gem on the bosom of a virgin wilderness. The "fir trees, the pine trees, and the bay," rejoice together in freedom, for as yet the axe has spared them; in the noble bay no shipping has found shelter; no voice or sound of civilized man has broken the sweet calm of the forest. The oak leaves, now turned to crimson and maroon by the autumn frosts, reflect themselves in flushes of color on the still waters. The golden leaves of the sassafras yet cling to the branches, though their life has passed, and every brushing wind bears showers of them down to the water. Here and there the dark spires of the cedar and the green leaves and red berries of the holly contrast with these lighter tints. The forest foliage grows down to the water's edge, so that the dash of the rising and falling tide washes into the shaggy cedar boughs which here and there lean over and dip in the waves.

No voice or sound from earth or sky proclaims that anything unwonted is coming or doing on these shores to-day. The wandering Indians, moving their hunting-camps along the woodland paths, saw no sign in the stars that morning, and no different color in the sunrise from what had been in the days of their fathers. Panther and wild-cat under their furry coats felt no thrill of coming dispossession, and saw nothing through their great golden eyes but the dawning of a day just like all other days--when "the sun ariseth and they gather themselves into their dens and lay them down." And yet alike to Indian, panther, and wild-cat, to every oak of the forest, to every foot of land in America, from the stormy Atlantic to the broad Pacific, that day was a day of days.

There had been stormy and windy weather, but now dawned on the earth one of those still, golden times of November, full of dreamy rest and tender calm. The skies above were blue and fair, and the waters of the curving bay were a downward sky--a magical under-world, wherein the crimson oaks, and the dusk plumage of the pine, and the red holly-berries, and yellow sassafras leaves, all flickered and glinted in wavering bands of color as soft winds swayed the glassy floor of waters.

In a moment, there is heard in the silent bay a sound of a rush and ripple, different from the lap of the many-tongued waves on the shore; and, silently as a cloud, with white wings spread, a little vessel glides into the harbor.

A little craft is she--not larger than the fishing-smacks that ply their course along our coasts in summer; but her decks are crowded with men, women, and children, looking out with joyous curiosity on the beautiful bay, where, after many dangers and storms, they first have found safe shelter and hopeful harbor.

That small, unknown ship was the ***Mayflower;*** those men and women who crowded her decks were that little handful of God's own wheat which had been flailed by adversity, tossed and winnowed till every husk of earthly selfishness and self-will had been beaten away from them and left only pure seed, fit for the planting of a new world. It was old Master Cotton Mather who said of them, "The Lord sifted three countries to find seed wherewith to plant America."

Hark now to the hearty cry of the sailors, as with a plash and a cheer the anchor goes down, just in the deep water inside of Long Point; and then, says their journal, "being now passed the vast ocean and sea of troubles, before their preparation unto further proceedings as to seek out a place for habitation, they fell down on their knees and blessed the Lord, the God of heaven, who had brought them over the vast and furious ocean, and delivered them from all perils and miseries thereof."

Let us draw nigh and mingle with this singular act of worship. Elder Brewster, with his well-worn Geneva Bible in hand, leads the thanksgiving in words which, though thousands of years old, seem as if written for the occasion of that hour:

"Praise the Lord because he is good, for his mercy endureth forever. Let them which have been redeemed of the Lord show how he delivereth them from the hand of the oppressor, And gathered them out of the lands: from the east, and from the west, from the north, and from the south, when they wandered in deserts and wildernesses out of the way and found no city to dwell in. Both hungry and thirsty, their soul failed in them. Then they cried unto the Lord in their troubles, and he delivered them in their distresses. And led them forth by the right way, that they might go unto a city of habitation. They that go down to the sea and occupy by the great waters: they see the works of the Lord and his wonders in the deep. For he commandeth and raiseth the stormy wind, and it lifteth up the waves thereof. They mount up to heaven, and descend to the deep: so that their soul melteth for trouble. They are tossed to and fro, and stagger like a drunken man, and all their cunning is gone. Then they cry unto the Lord in their trouble, and he bringeth them out of their distresses. He turneth the storm to a calm, so that the waves thereof are still. When they are quieted they are glad, and he bringeth them unto the haven where they would be."

As yet, the treasures of sacred song which are the liturgy of modern Christians had not arisen in the church. There was no Watts, and no Wesley, in the days of the Pilgrims; they brought with them in each family, as the most precious of household possessions, a thick volume containing, first, the Book of Common Prayer, with the Psalter appointed to be read in churches; second, the whole Bible in the Geneva translation, which was the basis on which our present English translation was made; and, third, the Psalms of David, in meter, by Sternhold and Hopkins, with the music notes of the tunes, adapted to singing. Therefore it was that our little band were able to lift up their voices together in song and that the noble tones of Old Hundred for the first time floated over the silent bay and mingled with the sound of winds and waters, consecrating our American shores.

"All people that on earth do dwell,
  Sing to the Lord with cheerful voice:
Him serve with fear, His praise forthtell;
  Come ye before Him and rejoice.

"The Lord, ye know, is God indeed;
  Without our aid He did us make;
We are His flock, He doth us feed,
  And for his sheep He doth us take.

"O enter then His gates with praise,
  Approach with joy His courts unto:
Praise, laud, and bless His name always,
  For it is seemly so to do.

"For why? The Lord our God is good,
  His mercy is forever sure;
His truth at all times firmly stood,
  And shall from age to age endure."

This grand hymn rose and swelled and vibrated in the still November air; while in between the pauses came the warble of birds, the scream of the jay, the hoarse call of hawk and eagle, going on with their forest ways all unmindful of the new era which had been ushered in with those solemn sounds.

CHAPTER II.
THE FIRST DAY ON SHORE.

The sound of prayer and psalm-singing died away on the shore, and the little band, rising from their knees, saluted each other in that genial humor which always possesses a ship's company when they have weathered the ocean and come to land together.

"Well, Master Jones, here we' are," said Elder Brewster cheerily to the ship-master.

"Aye, aye, sir, here we be sure enough; but I've had many a shrewd doubt of this upshot. I tell you, sirs, when that beam amidships sprung and cracked Master Coppin here said we must give over--hands couldn't bring her through. Thou rememberest, Master Coppin?"

"That I do," replied Master Coppin, the first mate, a stocky, cheery sailor, with a face red and shining as a glazed bun. "I said then that praying might save her, perhaps, but nothing else would."

"Praying wouldn't have saved her," said Master Brown, the carpenter, "if I had not put in that screw and worked the beam to her place again."

"Aye, aye, Master Carpenter," said Elder Brewster, "the Lord hath abundance of the needful ever to his hand. When He wills to answer prayer, there will be found both carpenter and screws in their season, I trow."

"Well, Deb," said Master Coppin, pinching the ear of a great mastiff bitch who sat by him, "what sayest thou? Give us thy mind on it, old girl; say, wilt thou go deer-hunting with us yonder?"

The dog, who was full of the excitement of all around, wagged her tail and gave three tremendous barks, whereat a little spaniel with curly ears, that stood by Rose Standish, barked aloud.

"Well done!" said Captain Miles Standish. "Why, here is a salute of ordnance! Old Deb is in the spirit of the thing and opens out like a cannon. The old girl is spoiling for a chase in those woods."

"Father, may I go ashore? I want to see the country," said Wrestling Brewster, a bright, sturdy boy, creeping up to Elder Brewster and touching his father's elbow.

Thereat there was a crying to the different mothers of girls and boys tired of being cooped up,--"Oh, mother, mother, ask that we may all go ashore."

"For my part," said old Margery the serving-maid to Elder Brewster, "I want to go ashore to wash and be decent, for there isn't a soul of us hath anything fit for Christians. There be springs of water, I trow."

"Never doubt it, my woman," said Elder Brewster; "but all things in their order. How say you, Mr. Carver? You are our governor. What order shall we take?"

"We must have up the shallop," said Carver, "and send a picked company to see what entertainment there may be for us on shore."

"And I counsel that all go well armed," quoth Captain Miles Standish, "for these men of the forest are sharper than a thorn-hedge. What! what!" he said, looking over to the eager group of girls and boys, "ye would go ashore, would ye? Why, the lions and bears will make one mouthful of ye."

"I'm not afraid of lions," said young Wrestling Brewster in an aside to little Love Winslow, a golden-haired, pale-cheeked child, of a tender and spiritual beauty of face. "I'd like to meet a lion," he added, "and serve him as Samson did. I'd get honey out of him, I promise."

"Oh, there you are, young Master Boastful!" said old Margery. "Mind the old saying, 'Brag is a good dog, but holdfast is better.'"

"Dear husband," said Rose Standish, "wilt thou go ashore in this company?"

"Why, aye, sweetheart, what else am I come for--and who should go if not I?"

"Thou art so very venturesome, Miles."

"Even so, my Rose of the wilderness. Why else am I come on this quest? Not being good enough to be in your church nor one of the saints, I come for an arm of flesh to them, and so, here goes on my armor."

And as he spoke, he buried his frank, good-natured countenance in an iron headpiece, and Rose hastened to help him adjust his corselet.

The clang of armor, the bustle and motion of men and children, the barking of dogs, and the cheery Heave-o! of the sailors marked the setting off of the party which comprised some of the gravest, and wisest, as well as the youngest and most able-bodied of the ship's' company. The impatient children ran in a group and clustered on the side of the ship to see them go. Old Deb, with her two half-grown pups, barked and yelped after her master in the boat, running up and down the vessel's deck with piteous cries of impatience.

"Come hither, dear old Deb," said little Love Winslow, running up and throwing her arms round the dog's rough neck; "thou must not take on so; thy master will be back again; so be a good dog now, and lie down."

And the great rough mastiff quieted down under her caresses, and sitting down by her she patted and played with her, with her little thin hands.

"See the darling," said Rose Standish, "what away that baby hath! In all the roughness and the terrors of the sea she hath been like a little sunbeam to us--yet she is so frail!"

"She hath been marked in the womb by the troubles her mother bore," said old Margery, shaking her head. "She never had the ways of other babies, but hath ever that wistful look--and her eyes are brighter than they should be. Mistress Winslow will never raise that child--now mark me!"

"Take care!" said Rose, "let not her mother hear you."

"Why, look at her beside of Wrestling Brewster, or Faith Carver. They are flesh and blood, and she looks as if she had been made out of sunshine. 'Tis a sweet babe as ever was; but fitter for the kingdom of heaven than our rough life--deary me! a hard time we have had of it. I suppose it's all best, but I don't know."

"Oh, never talk that way, Margery," said Rose Standish; "we must all keep up heart, our own and one another's."

"Ah, well a day--I suppose so, but then I look at my good Master Brewster and remember how, when I was a girl, he was at our good Queen Elizabeth's court, ruffling it with the best, and everybody said that there wasn't a young man that had good fortune to equal his. Why, Master Davidson, the Queen's Secretary of State, thought all the world of him; and when he went to Holland on the Queen's business, he must take him along; and when he took the keys of the cities there, it was my master that he trusted them to, who used to sleep with them under his pillow. I remember when he came home to the Queen's court, wearing the great gold chain that the States had given him. Ah me! I little thought he would ever come to a poor man's coat, then!"

"Well, good Margery," said Rose, "it isn't the coat, but the heart under it--that's the thing. Thou hast more cause of pride in thy master's poverty than in his riches."

"Maybe so--I don't know," said Margery, "but he hath had many a sore trouble in worldly things--driven and hunted from place to place in England, clapt into prison, and all he had eaten up with fines and charges and costs."

"All that is because he chose rather to suffer affliction with the people of God than to enjoy the pleasures of sin for a season," said Rose; "he shall have his reward by and by."

"Well, there be good men and godly in Old England that get to heaven in better coats and with easy carriages and fine houses and servants, and I would my master had been of such. But if he must come to the wilderness I will come with him. Gracious me! what noise is that?" she exclaimed, as a sudden report of firearms from below struck her ear. "I do believe there is that Frank Billington at the gunpowder; that boy will never leave, I do believe, till he hath blown up the ship's company."

In fact, it appeared that young master Frank, impatient of the absence of his father, had toled Wrestling Brewster and two other of the boys down into the cabin to show them his skill in managing his father's fowling- piece, had burst the gun, scattering the pieces about the cabin.

Margery soon appeared, dragging the culprit after her. "Look here now, Master Malapert, see what you'll get when your father comes home! Lord a mercy! here was half a keg of powder standing open! Enough to have blown us all up! Here, Master Clarke, Master Clarke, come and keep this boy with you till his father come back, or we be all sent sky high before we know."

*   *   *   *   *

At even tide the boat came back laden to the water's edge with the first gettings and givings from the new soil of America. There is a richness and sweetness gleaming through the brief records of these men in their journals, which shows how the new land was seen through a fond and tender medium, half poetic; and its new products lend a savor to them of somewhat foreign and rare.

Of this day's expedition the record is thus:

"That day, so soon as we could, we set ashore some fifteen or sixteen men well armed, with some to fetch wood, for we had none left; as also to see what the land was and what inhabitants they could meet with. They found it to be a small neck of land on this side where we lay in the bay, and on the further side the sea, the ground or earth, sand-hills, much like the downs in Holland, but much better; the crust of the earth a spit's depth of excellent black earth; all wooded with oaks, pines, sassafras, juniper, birch, holly, vines, some ash and walnut; the wood for the most part open and without underwood, fit either to walk or to ride in. At night our people returned and found not any people or inhabitants, and laded their boat with juniper, which smelled very sweet and strong, and of which we burned for the most part while we were there."

"See there," said little Love Winslow, "what fine red berries Captain Miles Standish hath brought."

"Yea, my little maid, there is a brave lot of holly berries for thee to dress the cabin withal. We shall not want for Christmas greens here, though the houses and churches are yet to come."

"Yea, Brother Miles," said Elder Brewster, "the trees of the Lord are full of sap in this land, even the cedars of Lebanon, which he hath planted. It hath the look to me of a land which the Lord our God hath blessed."

"There is a most excellent depth of black, rich earth," said Carver, "and a great tangle of grapevines, whereon the leaves in many places yet hung, and we picked up stores of walnuts under a tree--not so big as our English ones--but sweet and well-flavored."

"Know ye, brethren, what in this land smelleth sweetest to me?" said Elder Brewster. "It is the smell of liberty. The soil is free--no man hath claim thereon. In Old England a poor man may starve right on his mother's bosom; there may be stores of fish in the river, and bird and fowl flying, and deer running by, and yet though a man's children be crying for bread, an' he catch a fish or snare a bird, he shall be snatched up and hanged. This is a sore evil in Old England; but we will make a country here for the poor to dwell in, where the wild fruits and fish and fowl shall be the inheritance of whosoever will have them; and every man shall have his portion of our good mother earth, with no lords and no bishops to harry and distrain, and worry with taxes and tythes."

"Amen, brother!" said Miles Standish, "and thereto I give my best endeavors with sword and buckler."

CHAPTER III.
CHRISTMAS TIDE IN PLYMOUTH HARBOR.

For the rest of that month of November the ***Mayflower*** lay at anchor in Cape Cod harbor, and formed a floating home for the women and children, while the men were out exploring the country, with a careful and steady shrewdness and good sense, to determine where should be the site of the future colony. The record of their adventures is given in their journals with that sweet homeliness of phrase which hangs about the Old English of that period like the smell of rosemary in an ancient cabinet.

We are told of a sort of picnic day, when "our women went on shore to wash and all to refresh themselves;" and fancy the times there must have been among the little company, while the mothers sorted and washed and dried the linen, and the children, under the keeping of the old mastiffs and with many cautions against the wolves and wild cubs, once more had liberty to play in the green wood. For it appears in these journals how, in one case, the little spaniel of John Goodman was chased by two wolves, and was fain to take refuge between his master's legs for shelter. Goodman "had nothing in hand," says the journal, "but took up a stick and threw at one of them and hit him, and they presently ran away, but came again. He got a pale-board in his hand, but they both sat on their tails a good while, grinning at him, and then went their way and left him."

Such little touches show what the care of families must have been in the woodland picnics, and why the ship was, on the whole, the safest refuge for the women and children.

We are told, moreover, how the party who had struck off into the wilderness, "having marched through boughs and bushes and under hills and valleys which tore our very armor in pieces, yet could meet with no inhabitants nor find any fresh water which we greatly stood in need of, for we brought neither beer nor water with us, and our victual was only biscuit and Holland cheese, and a little bottle of aqua vitae. So we were sore athirst. About ten o'clock we came into a deep valley full of brush, sweet gaile and long grass, through which we found little paths or tracks; and we saw there a deer and found springs of water, of which we were heartily glad, and sat us down and drunk our first New England water with as much delight as we ever drunk drink in all our lives."

Three such expeditions through the country, with all sorts of haps and mishaps and adventures, took up the time until near the 15th of December, when, having selected a spot for their colony, they weighed anchor to go to their future home.

Plymouth Harbor, as they found it, is thus described:

"This harbor is a bay greater than Cape Cod, compassed with a goodly land, and in the bay two fine islands uninhabited, wherein are nothing but woods, oaks, pines, walnuts, beeches, sassafras, vines, and other trees which we know not. The bay is a most hopeful place, innumerable stores of fowl, and excellent good; and it cannot but be of fish in their season. Skate, cod, and turbot, and herring we have tasted of--abundance of mussels (clams) the best we ever saw; and crabs and lobsters in their time, infinite."

On the main land they write:

"The land is, for a spit's depth, excellent black mould and fat in some places. Two or three great oaks, pines, walnut, beech, ash, birch, hazel, holly, and sassafras in abundance, and vines everywhere, with cherry- trees, plum-trees, and others which we know not. Many kind of herbs we found here in winter, as strawberry leaves innumerable, sorrel, yarrow, carvel, brook-lime, liver-wort, water-cresses, with great store of leeks and onions, and an excellent strong kind of flax and hemp."

It is evident from this description that the season was a mild one even thus late into December, that there was still sufficient foliage hanging upon the trees to determine the species, and that the pilgrims viewed their new mother-land through eyes of cheerful hope.

And now let us look in the glass at them once more, on Saturday morning of the 23d of December.

The little *Mayflower* lies swinging at her moorings in the harbor, while every man and boy who could use a tool has gone on shore to cut down and prepare timber for future houses.

Mary Winslow and Rose Standish are sitting together on deck, fashioning garments, while little Love Winslow is playing at their feet with such toys as the new world afforded her--strings of acorns and scarlet holly- berries and some bird-claws and arrowheads and bright-colored ears of Indian corn, which Captain Miles Standish has brought home to her from one of their explorations.

Through the still autumnal air may now and then be heard the voices of men calling to one another on shore, the quick, sharp ring of axes, and anon the crash of falling trees, with shouts from juveniles as the great forest monarch is laid low. Some of the women are busy below, sorting over and arranging their little house-hold stores and stuff with a view to moving on shore, and holding domestic consultations with each other.

A sadness hangs over the little company, for since their arrival the stroke of death has more than once fallen; we find in Bradford's brief record that by the 24th of December six had died.

What came nearest to the hearts of all was the loss of Dorothea Bradford, who, when all the men of the party were absent on an exploring tour, accidentally fell over the side of the vessel and sunk in the deep waters. What this loss was to the husband and the little company of brothers and sisters appears by no note or word of wailing, merely by a simple entry which says no more than the record on a grave-stone, that, "on the 7th of December, Dorothy, wife of William Bradford, fell over and was drowned."

That much-enduring company could afford themselves few tears. Earthly having and enjoying was a thing long since dismissed from their calculations. They were living on the primitive Christian platform; they "rejoiced as though they rejoiced not," and they "wept as though they wept not," and they "had wives and children as though they had them not," or, as one of themselves expressed it, "We are in all places strangers, pilgrims, travelers and sojourners; our dwelling is but a wandering, our abiding but as a fleeting, our home is nowhere but in the heavens, in that house not made with hands, whose builder and maker is God."

When one of their number fell they were forced to do as soldiers in the stress of battle--close up the ranks and press on.

But Mary Winslow, as she sat over her sewing, dropped now and then a tear down on her work for the loss of her sister and counselor and long-tried friend. From the lower part of the ship floated up, at intervals, snatches of an old English ditty that Margery was singing while she moved to and fro about her work, one of those genuine English melodies, full of a rich, strange mournfulness blent with a soothing pathos:

"Fear no more the heat o' the sun
  Nor the furious winter rages,
Thou thy worldly task hast done,
  Home art gone and ta'en thy wages."

The air was familiar, and Mary Winslow, dropping her work in her lap, involuntarily joined in it:

"Fear no more the frown of the great,
  Thou art past the tyrant's stroke;
Care no more to clothe and eat,
  To thee the reed is as the oak."

"There goes a great tree on shore!" quoth little Love Winslow, clapping her hands. "Dost hear, mother? I've been counting the strokes--fifteen-- and then crackle! crackle! crackle! and down it comes!"

"Peace, darling," said Mary Winslow; "hear what old Margery is singing below:

"Fear no more the lightning's flash,
  Nor the all-dreaded thunder stone;
Fear not slander, censure rash--
  Thou hast finished joy and moan.
All lovers young--all lovers must
  Consign to thee, and come to dust."

"Why do you cry, mother?" said the little one, climbing on her lap and wiping her tears.

"I was thinking of dear Auntie, who is gone from us."

"She is not gone from us, mother."

"My darling, she is with Jesus."

"Well, mother, Jesus is ever with us--you tell me that--and if she is with him she is with us too--I know she is--for sometimes I see her. She sat by me last night and stroked my head when that ugly, stormy wind waked me--she looked so sweet, oh, ever so beautiful!--and she made me go to sleep so quiet--it is sweet to be as she is, mother--not away from us but with Jesus."

"These little ones see further in the kingdom than we," said Rose Standish. "If we would be like them, we should take things easier. When the Lord would show who was greatest in his kingdom, he took a little child on his lap."

"Ah me, Rose!" said Mary Winslow, "I am aweary in spirit with this tossing sea-life. I long to have a home on dry land once more, be it ever so poor. The sea wearies me. Only think, it is almost Christmas time, only two days now to Christmas. How shall we keep it in these woods?"

"Aye, aye," said old Margery, coming up at the moment, "a brave muster and to do is there now in old England; and men and boys going forth singing and bearing home branches of holly, and pine, and mistletoe for Christmas greens. Oh! I remember I used to go forth with them and help dress the churches. God help the poor children, they will grow up in the wilderness and never see such brave sights as I have. They will never know what a church is, such as they are in old England, with fine old windows like the clouds, and rainbows, and great wonderful arches like the very skies above us, and the brave music with the old organs rolling and the boys marching in white garments and singing so as should draw the very heart out of one. All this we have left behind in old England--ah! well a day! well a day!"

"Oh, but, Margery," said Mary Winslow, "we have a 'better country' than old England, where the saints and angels are keeping Christmas; we confess that we are strangers and pilgrims on earth."

And Rose Standish immediately added the familiar quotation from the Geneva Bible:

"For they that say such things declare plainly that they seek a country. For if they had been mindful of that country from whence they came out they had leisure to have returned. But now they desire a better--that is, an heavenly; wherefore God is not ashamed of them to be called their God."

The fair young face glowed as she repeated the heroic words, for already, though she knew it not, Rose Standish was feeling the approaching sphere of the angel life. Strong in spirit, as delicate in frame, she had given herself and drawn her martial husband to the support of a great and noble cause; but while the spirit was ready, the flesh was weak, and even at that moment her name was written in the Lamb's Book to enter the higher life, in one short month's time from that Christmas.

Only one month of sweetness and perfume was that sweet rose to shed over the hard and troubled life of the pilgrims, for the saints and angels loved her, and were from day to day gently untying mortal bands to draw her to themselves. Yet was there nothing about her of mournfulness; on the contrary, she was ever alert and bright, with a ready tongue to cheer and a helpful hand to do; and, seeing the sadness that seemed stealing over Mary Winslow, she struck another key, and, catching little Love up in her arms, said cheerily,

"Come hither, pretty one, and Rose will sing thee a brave carol for Christmas. We won't be down-hearted, will we? Hark now to what the minstrels used to sing under my window when I was a little girl:

"I saw three ships come sailing in On Christmas day, on Christmas day, I saw three ships come sailing in On Christmas day in the morning.

"And what was in those ships all three On Christmas day, on Christmas day, And what was in those ships all three On Christmas day in the morning?

"Our Saviour Christ and his laydie, On Christmas day, on Christmas day, Our Saviour Christ and his laydie On Christmas day in the morning.

"Pray, whither sailed those ships all three, On Christmas day, on Christmas day? Oh, they sailed into Bethlehem, On Christmas day in the morning.

"And all the bells on earth shall ring On Christmas day, on Christmas day; And all the angels in heaven shall sing On Christmas day in the morning.

"Then let us all rejoice amain, On Christmas day, on Christmas day; Then let us all rejoice amain On Christmas day in the morning."

"Now, isn't that a brave ballad?" said Rose. "Yea, and thou singest like a real English robin," said Margery, "to do the heart good to hear thee."

CHAPTER IV.
ELDER BREWSTER'S CHRISTMAS SERMON.

Sunday morning found the little company gathered once more on the ship, with nothing to do but rest and remember their homes, temporal and spiritual-- homes backward, in old England, and forward, in Heaven. They were, every man and woman of them, English to the back-bone. From Captain Jones who command- ed the ship to Elder Brewster who ruled and guided in spiritual affairs, all alike were of that stock and breeding which made the Englishman of the days of Bacon and Shakespeare, and in those days Christmas was knit into the heart of every one of them by a thousand threads, which no after years could untie.

Christmas carols had been sung to them by nurses and mothers and grand- mothers; the Christmas holly spoke to them from every berry and prickly leaf, full of dearest household memories. Some of them had been men of substance among the English gentry, and in their prosperous days had held high festival in ancestral halls in the season of good cheer. Elder Brewster himself had been a rising young diplomat in the court of Elizabeth, in the days when the Lord Keeper of the Seals led the revels of Christmas as Lord of Misrule.

So that, though this Sunday morning arose gray and lowering, with snow- flakes hovering through the air, there was Christmas in the thoughts of every man and woman among them--albeit it was the Christmas of wanderers and exiles in a wilderness looking back to bright home-fires across stormy waters.

The men had come back from their work on shore with branches of green pine and holly, and the women had, stuck them about the ship, not without tearful thoughts of old home-places, where their childhood fathers and mothers did the same.

Bits and snatches of Christmas carols were floating all around the ship, like land-birds blown far out to sea. In the forecastle Master Coppin was singing:

"Come, bring with a noise,
  My merry boys,

The Christmas log to the firing;
While my good dame, she
Bids ye all be free,
  And drink to your hearts' desiring.
Drink now the strong beer,
Cut the white loaf here.
  The while the meat is shredding
For the rare minced pie,
And the plums stand by
  To fill the paste that's a-kneading."

"Ah, well-a-day, Master Jones, it is dull cheer to sing Christmas songs here in the woods, with only the owls and the bears for choristers. I wish I could hear the bells of merry England once more."

And down in the cabin Rose Standish was hushing little Peregrine, the first American-born baby, with a Christmas lullaby:

"This winter's night
I saw a sight--
  A star as bright as day;
And ever among
A maiden sung,
  Lullay, by-by, lullay!

"This lovely laydie sat and sung,
  And to her child she said,
My son, my brother, and my father dear,
  Why lyest thou thus in hayd?
My sweet bird,
Tho' it betide
  Thou be not king veray;
But nevertheless

I will not cease
  To sing, by-by, lullay!

"The child then spake in his talking,
  And to his mother he said,
It happeneth, mother, I am a king,
  In crib though I be laid,
For angels bright
Did down alight,
  Thou knowest it is no nay;
And of that sight
Thou may'st be light
  To sing, by-by, lullay!

"Now, sweet son, since thou art a king,
  Why art thou laid in stall?
Why not ordain thy bedding
  In some great king his hall?
We thinketh 'tis right
That king or knight
  Should be in good array;
And them among,
It were no wrong
  To sing, by-by, lullay!

"Mary, mother, I am thy child,
  Tho' I be laid in stall;
Lords and dukes shall worship me,
  And so shall kinges all.
And ye shall see
That kinges three
  Shall come on the twelfth day;
For this behest

Give me thy breast,
  And sing, by-by, lullay!"

"See here," quoth Miles Standish, "when my Rose singeth, the children gather round her like bees round a flower. Come, let us all strike up a goodly carol together. Sing one, sing all, girls and boys, and get a bit of Old England's Christmas before to-morrow, when we must to our work on shore."

Thereat Rose struck up a familiar ballad-meter of a catching rhythm, and every voice of young and old was soon joining in it:

"Behold a silly,[1] tender Babe,
In freezing winter night, In homely manger trembling lies;
Alas! a piteous sight, The inns are full, no man will yield
This little Pilgrim bed; But forced He is, with silly beasts
In crib to shroud His head. Despise Him not for lying there,
First what He is inquire: An orient pearl is often found
In depth of dirty mire.

"Weigh not His crib, His wooden dish,
Nor beasts that by Him feed; Weigh not His mother's poor attire,
Nor Joseph's simple weed. This stable is a Prince's court,
The crib His chair of state, The beasts are parcel of His pomp,
The wooden dish His plate. The persons in that poor attire
His royal liveries wear; The Prince Himself is come from Heaven,
This pomp is prized there. With joy approach, O Christian wight,
Do homage to thy King; And highly praise His humble pomp,
Which He from Heaven doth bring."

The cheerful sounds spread themselves through the ship like the flavor of some rare perfume, bringing softness of heart through a thousand tender memories.

Anon, the hour of Sabbath morning worship drew on, and Elder Brewster read from the New Testament the whole story of the Nativity, and then gave a sort of

---

1 Old English--simple.

Christmas homily from the words of St. Paul, in the eighth chapter of Romans, the sixth and seventh verses, which the Geneva version thus renders:

"For the wisdom of the flesh is death, but the wisdom of the spirit is life and peace.

"For the wisdom of the flesh is enmity against God, for it is not subject to the law of God, neither indeed can be."

"Ye know full well, dear brethren, what the wisdom of the flesh sayeth. The wisdom of the flesh sayeth to each one, 'Take care of thyself; look after thyself, to get and to have and to hold and to enjoy.' The wisdom of the flesh sayeth, 'So thou art warm, full, and in good liking, take thine ease, eat, drink, and be merry, and care not how many go empty and be lacking.' But ye have seen in the Gospel this morning that this was not the wisdom of our Lord Jesus Christ, who, though he was Lord of all, became poorer than any, that we, through His poverty, might become rich. When our Lord Jesus Christ came, the wisdom of the flesh despised Him; the wisdom of the flesh had no room for Him at the inn.

"There was room enough always for Herod and his concubines, for the wisdom of the flesh set great store by them; but a poor man and woman were thrust out to a stable; and *there* was a poor baby born whom the wisdom of the flesh knew not, because the wisdom of the flesh is enmity against God.

"The wisdom of the flesh, brethren, ever despiseth the wisdom of God, because it knoweth it not. The wisdom of the flesh looketh at the thing that is great and strong and high; it looketh at riches, at kings' courts, at fine clothes and fine jewels and fine feastings, and it despiseth the little and the poor and the weak.

"But the wisdom of the Spirit goeth to worship the poor babe in the manger, and layeth gold and myrrh and frankincense at his feet while he lieth in weakness and poverty, as did the wise men who were taught of God.

"Now, forasmuch as our Saviour Christ left His riches and throne in glory and came in weakness and poverty to this world, that he might work out a mighty salvation that shall be to all people, how can we better keep Christmas than to follow in his steps? We be a little company who have forsaken houses and lands and possessions, and come here unto the wilderness that we may prepare a resting-place whereto others shall come to reap what we shall sow. And to-morrow we shall keep our first Christmas, not in flesh-pleasing, and in reveling and in fullness of bread, but in small beginning and great weakness, as our Lord Christ kept it when He was born in a stable and lay in a manger.

"To-morrow, God willing, we will all go forth to do good, honest Christian work, and begin the first house-building in this our New England--it may be roughly fashioned, but as good a house, I'll warrant me, as our Lord Christ had on the Christmas Day we wot of. And let us not faint in heart because the wisdom of the world despiseth what we do. Though Sanballat the Horonite, and Tobias the Ammonite, and Geshem the Arabian make scorn of us, and say, 'What do these weak Jews? If a fox go up, he shall break down their stone wall;' yet the Lord our God is with us, and He can cause our work to prosper.

"The wisdom of the Spirit seeth the grain of mustard-seed, that is the least of all seeds, how it shall become a great tree, and the fowls of heaven shall lodge in its branches. Let us, then, lift up the hands that hang down and the feeble knees, and let us hope that, like as great salvation to all people came out of small beginnings of Bethlehem, so the work which we shall begin to-morrow shall be for the good of many nations.

"It is a custom on this Christmas Day to give love-presents. What love- gift giveth our Lord Jesus on this day? Brethren, it is a great one and a precious; as St. Paul said to the Philippians: 'For unto you it is given for Christ, not only that ye should believe on Him, but also that ye should suffer for His sake;' and St. Peter also saith, 'Behold, we count them blessed which endure.' And the holy Apostles rejoiced that they were counted worthy to suffer rebuke for the name of Jesus.

"Our Lord Christ giveth us of His cup and His baptism; He giveth of the manger and the straw; He giveth of persecutions and afflictions; He giveth of the crown of thorns, and right dear unto us be these gifts.

"And now will I tell these children a story, which a cunning playwright, whom I once knew in our Queen's court, hath made concerning gifts:

"A great king would marry his daughter worthily, and so he caused three caskets to be made, in one of which he hid her picture. The one casket was of gold set with diamonds, the second of silver set with pearls, and the third a poor casket of lead.

"Now it was given out that each comer should have but one choice, and if he chose the one with the picture he should have the lady to wife.

"Divers kings, knights, and gentlemen came from far, but they never won, because they always snatched at the gold and the silver caskets, with the pearls and diamonds. So, when they opened these, they found only a grinning death's-head or a fool's cap.

"But anon cometh a true, brave knight and gentleman, who chooseth for love alone the old leaden casket; and, behold, within is the picture of her he loveth! and they were married with great feasting and content.

"So our Lord Jesus doth not offer himself to us in silver and gold and jewels, but in poverty and hardness and want; but whoso chooseth them for His love's sake shall find Him therein whom his soul loveth, and shall enter with joy to the marriage supper of the Lamb.

"And when the Lord shall come again in his glory, then he shall bring worthy gifts with him, for he saith: 'Be thou faithful unto death, and I will give thee a crown of life; to him that overcometh I will give to eat of the hidden manna, and I will give him a white stone with a new name that no man knoweth save he that receiveth it. He that overcometh and keepeth my words, I will give power over the nations and I will give him the morning star.'

"Let us then take joyfully Christ's Christmas gifts of labors and adversities and crosses to-day, that when he shall appear we may have these great and wonderful gifts at his coming; for if we suffer with him we shall also reign; but if we deny him, he also will deny us."

And so it happens that the only record of Christmas Day in the pilgrims' journal is this:

"Monday, the 25th, being Christmas Day, we went ashore, some to fell timber, some to saw, some to rive, and some to carry; and so no man rested all that day. But towards night some, as they were at work, heard a noise of Indians, which caused us all to go to our muskets; but we heard no further, so we came aboard again, leaving some to keep guard. That night we had a sore storm of wind and rain. But at night the ship- master caused us to have some beer aboard."

So worthily kept they the first Christmas, from which comes all the Christmas cheer of New England to-day. There is no record how Mary Winslow and Rose Standish and others, with women and children, came ashore and walked about encouraging the builders; and how little Love gathered stores of bright checker-berries and partridge plums, and was made merry in seeing squirrels and wild rabbits; nor how old Margery roasted certain wild geese to a turn at a woodland fire, and conserved wild cranberries with honey for sauce. In their journals the good pilgrims say they found bushels of strawberries in the meadows in December. But we, knowing the nature of things, know that these must have been cranberries, which grow still abundantly around Plymouth harbor.

And at the very time that all this was doing in the wilderness, and the men were working yeomanly to build a new nation, in King James's court the ambassadors of the French King were being entertained with maskings and mummerings, wherein the staple subject of merriment was the Puritans!

So goes the wisdom of the world and its ways--and so goes the wisdom of God!

The Codes Of Hammurabi And Moses
W. W. Davies

QTY

The discovery of the Hammurabi Code is one of the greatest achievements of archaeology, and is of paramount interest, not only to the student of the Bible, but also to all those interested in ancient history...

Religion   **ISBN:** *1-59462-338-4*   **Pages:132**
MSRP $12.95

The Theory of Moral Sentiments
Adam Smith

QTY

This work from 1749. contains original theories of conscience amd moral judgment and it is the foundation for systemof morals.

Philosophy **ISBN:** *1-59462-777-0*   **Pages:536**
MSRP $19.95

Jessica's First Prayer
Hesba Stretton

QTY

In a screened and secluded corner of one of the many railway-bridges which span the streets of London there could be seen a few years ago, from five o'clock every morning until half past eight, a tidily set-out coffee-stall, consisting of a trestle and board, upon which stood two large tin cans, with a small fire of charcoal burning under each so as to keep the coffee boiling during the early hours of the morning when the work-people were thronging into the city on their way to their daily toil...

Pages:84

Childrens   **ISBN:** *1-59462-373-2*   *MSRP $9.95*

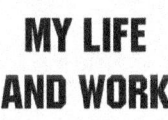

My Life and Work
Henry Ford

QTY

Henry Ford revolutionized the world with his implementation of mass production for the Model T automobile. Gain valuable business insight into his life and work with his own auto-biography... "We have only started on our development of our country we have not as yet, with all our talk of wonderful progress, done more than scratch the surface. The progress has been wonderful enough but..."

Pages:300

Biographies/   **ISBN:** *1-59462-198-5*   *MSRP $21.95*

The Art of Cross-Examination
Francis Wellman

QTY

I presume it is the experience of every author, after his first book is published upon an important subject, to be almost overwhelmed with a wealth of ideas and illustrations which could readily have been included in his book, and which to his own mind, at least, seem to make a second edition inevitable. Such certainly was the case with me; and when the first edition had reached its sixth impression in five months, I rejoiced to learn that it seemed to my publishers that the book had met with a sufficiently favorable reception to justify a second and considerably enlarged edition. ..

Pages:412

Reference   ISBN: *1-59462-647-2*   *MSRP $19.95*

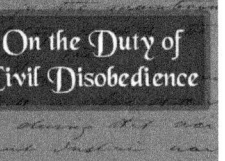

On the Duty of Civil Disobedience
Henry David Thoreau

QTY

Thoreau wrote his famous essay, On the Duty of Civil Disobedience, as a protest against an unjust but popular war and the immoral but popular institution of slave-owning. He did more than write—he declined to pay his taxes, and was hauled off to gaol in consequence. Who can say how much this refusal of his hastened the end of the war and of slavery ?

Law   ISBN: *1-59462-747-9*   **Pages:48**

MSRP $7.45

Dream Psychology Psychoanalysis for Beginners
Sigmund Freud

QTY

Sigmund Freud, born Sigismund Schlomo Freud (May 6, 1856 - September 23, 1939), was a Jewish-Austrian neurologist and psychiatrist who co-founded the psychoanalytic school of psychology. Freud is best known for his theories of the unconscious mind, especially involving the mechanism of repression; his redefinition of sexual desire as mobile and directed towards a wide variety of objects; and his therapeutic techniques, especially his understanding of transference in the therapeutic relationship and the presumed value of dreams as sources of insight into unconscious desires.

Pages:196

Psychology   ISBN: *1-59462-905-6*   *MSRP $15.45*

The Miracle of Right Thought
Orison Swett Marden

QTY

Believe with all of your heart that you will do what you were made to do. When the mind has once formed the habit of holding cheerful, happy, prosperous pictures, it will not be easy to form the opposite habit. It does not matter how improbable or how far away this realization may see, or how dark the prospects may be, if we visualize them as best we can, as vividly as possible, hold tenaciously to them and vigorously struggle to attain them, they will gradually become actualized, realized in the life. But a desire, a longing without endeavor, a yearning abandoned or held indifferently will vanish without realization.

Pages:360

Self Help   ISBN: *1-59462-644-8*   *MSRP $25.45*

QTY

The Rosicrucian Cosmo-Conception Mystic Christianity by *Max Heindel* ISBN: *1-59462-188-8* **$38.95**
The Rosicrucian Cosmo-conception is not dogmatic, neither does it appeal to any other authority than the reason of the student. It is: not controversial, but is: sent forth in the, hope that it may help to clear... New Age/Religion Pages 646

Abandonment To Divine Providence by *Jean-Pierre de Caussade* ISBN: *1-59462-228-0* **$25.95**
"The Rev. Jean Pierre de Caussade was one of the most remarkable spiritual writers of the Society of Jesus in France in the 18th Century. His death took place at Toulouse in 1751. His works have gone through many editions and have been republished... Inspirational/Religion Pages 400

Mental Chemistry by *Charles Haanel* ISBN: *1-59462-192-6* **$23.95**
Mental Chemistry allows the change of material conditions by combining and appropriately utilizing the power of the mind. Much like applied chemistry creates something new and unique out of careful combinations of chemicals the mastery of mental chemistry... New Age Pages 354

The Letters of Robert Browning and Elizabeth Barret Barrett 1845-1846 vol II ISBN: *1-59462-193-4* **$35.95**
by *Robert Browning* and *Elizabeth Barrett* Biographies Pages 596

Gleanings In Genesis (volume I) by *Arthur W. Pink* ISBN: *1-59462-130-6* **$27.45**
Appropriately has Genesis been termed "the seed plot of the Bible" for in it we have, in germ form, almost all of the great doctrines which are afterwards fully developed in the books of Scripture which follow... Religion/Inspirational Pages 420

The Master Key by *L. W. de Laurence* ISBN: *1-59462-001-6* **$30.95**
In no branch of human knowledge has there been a more lively increase of the spirit of research during the past few years than in the study of Psychology, Concentration and Mental Discipline. The requests for authentic lessons in Thought Control, Mental Discipline and... New Age/Business Pages 422

The Lesser Key Of Solomon Goetia by *L. W. de Laurence* ISBN: *1-59462-092-X* **$9.95**
This translation of the first book of the "Lernegton" which is now for the first time made accessible to students of Talismanic Magic was done, after careful collation and edition, from numerous Ancient Manuscripts in Hebrew, Latin, and French... New Age/Occult Pages 92

Rubaiyat Of Omar Khayyam by *Edward Fitzgerald* ISBN: *1-59462-332-5* **$13.95**
Edward Fitzgerald, whom the world has already learned, in spite of his own efforts to remain within the shadow of anonymity, to look upon as one of the rarest poets of the century, was born at Bredfield, in Suffolk, on the 31st of March, 1809. He was the third son of John Purcell... Music Pages 172

Ancient Law by *Henry Maine* ISBN: *1-59462-128-4* **$29.95**
The chief object of the following pages is to indicate some of the earliest ideas of mankind, as they are reflected in Ancient Law, and to point out the relation of those ideas to modern thought. Religion/History Pages 452

Far-Away Stories by *William J. Locke* ISBN: *1-59462-129-2* **$19.45**
"Good wine needs no bush, but a collection of mixed vintages does. And this book is just such a collection. Some of the stories I do not want to remain buried for ever in the museum files of dead magazine-numbers an author's not unpardonable vanity..." Fiction Pages 272

Life of David Crockett by *David Crockett* ISBN: *1-59462-250-7* **$27.45**
"Colonel David Crockett was one of the most remarkable men of the times in which he lived. Born in humble life, but gifted with a strong will, an indomitable courage, and unremitting perseverance... Biographies/New Age Pages 424

Lip-Reading by *Edward Nitchie* ISBN: *1-59462-206-X* **$25.95**
Edward B. Nitchie, founder of the New York School for the Hard of Hearing, now the Nitchie School of Lip-Reading, Inc, wrote "LIP-READING Principles and Practice". The development and perfecting of this meritorious work on lip-reading was an undertaking... How-to Pages 400

A Handbook of Suggestive Therapeutics, Applied Hypnotism, Psychic Science ISBN: *1-59462-214-0* **$24.95**
by *Henry Munro* Health/New Age/Health/Self-help Pages 376

A Doll's House: and Two Other Plays by *Henrik Ibsen* ISBN: *1-59462-112-8* **$19.95**
Henrik Ibsen created this classic when in revolutionary 1848 Rome. Introducing some striking concepts in playwriting for the realist genre, this play has been studied the world over. Fiction/Classics Plays 308

The Light of Asia by *sir Edwin Arnold* ISBN: *1-59462-204-3* **$13.95**
In this poetic masterpiece, Edwin Arnold describes the life and teachings of Buddha. The man who was to become known as Buddha to the world was born as Prince Gautama of India but he rejected the worldly riches and abandoned the reigns of power when... Religion/History/Biographies Pages 170

The Complete Works of Guy de Maupassant by *Guy de Maupassant* ISBN: *1-59462-157-8* **$16.95**
"For days and days, nights and nights, I had dreamed of that first kiss which was to consecrate our engagement, and I knew not on what spot I should put my lips..." Fiction/Classics Pages 240

The Art of Cross-Examination by *Francis L. Wellman* ISBN: *1-59462-309-0* **$26.95**
Written by a renowned trial lawyer, Wellman imparts his experience and uses case studies to explain how to use psychology to extract desired information through questioning. How-to/Science/Reference Pages 408

Answered or Unanswered? by *Louisa Vaughan* ISBN: *1-59462-248-5* **$10.95**
Miracles of Faith in China Religion Pages 112

The Edinburgh Lectures on Mental Science (1909) by *Thomas* ISBN: *1-59462-008-3* **$11.95**
This book contains the substance of a course of lectures recently given by the writer in the Queen Street Hall, Edinburgh. Its purpose is to indicate the Natural Principles governing the relation between Mental Action and Material Conditions... New Age/Psychology Pages 148

Ayesha by *H. Rider Haggard* ISBN: *1-59462-301-5* **$24.95**
Verily and indeed it is the unexpected that happens! Probably if there was one person upon the earth from whom the Editor of this, and of a certain previous history, did not expect to hear again... Classics Pages 380

Ayala's Angel by *Anthony Trollope* ISBN: *1-59462-352-X* **$29.95**
The two girls were both pretty, but Lucy who was twenty-one who supposed to be simple and comparatively unattractive, whereas Ayala was credited, as her Bombwhat romantic name might show, with poetic charm and a taste for romance. Ayala when her father died was nineteen... Fiction Pages 484

The American Commonwealth by *James Bryce* ISBN: *1-59462-286-8* **$34.45**
An interpretation of American democratic political theory. It examines political mechanics and society from the perspective of Scotsman James Bryce Politics Pages 572

Stories of the Pilgrims by *Margaret P. Pumphrey* ISBN: *1-59462-116-0* **$17.95**
This book explores pilgrims religious oppression in England as well as their escape to Holland and eventual crossing to America on the Mayflower, and their early days in New England... History Pages 268

QTY

The Fasting Cure *by Sinclair Upton*   ISBN: *1-59462-222-1*   **$13.95**
In the Cosmopolitan Magazine for May, 1910, and in the Contemporary Review (London) for April, 1910, I published an article dealing with my experiences in fasting. I have written a great many magazine articles, but never one which attracted so much attention... New Age/Self Help/Health Pages 164

Hebrew Astrology *by Sepharial*   ISBN: *1-59462-308-2*   **$13.45**
In these days of advanced thinking it is a matter of common observation that we have left many of the old landmarks behind and that we are now pressing forward to greater heights and to a wider horizon than that which represented the mind-content of our progenitors... Astrology Pages 144

Thought Vibration or The Law of Attraction in the Thought World   ISBN: *1-59462-127-6*   **$12.95**

by William Walker Atkinson   *Psychology/Religion Pages 144*

Optimism *by Helen Keller*   ISBN: *1-59462-108-X*   **$15.95**
Helen Keller was blind, deaf, and mute since 19 months old, yet famously learned how to overcome these handicaps, communicate with the world, and spread her lectures promoting optimism. An inspiring read for everyone... Biographies/Inspirational Pages 84

Sara Crewe *by Frances Burnett*   ISBN: *1-59462-360-0*   **$9.45**
In the first place, Miss Minchin lived in London. Her home was a large, dull, tall one, in a large, dull square, where all the houses were alike, and all the sparrows were alike, and where all the door-knockers made the same heavy sound... Childrens/Classic Pages 88

The Autobiography of Benjamin Franklin *by Benjamin Franklin*   ISBN: *1-59462-135-7*   **$24.95**
The Autobiography of Benjamin Franklin has probably been more extensively read than any other American historical work, and no other book of its kind has had such ups and downs of fortune. Franklin lived for many years in England, where he was agent... Biographies/History Pages 332

Name	
Email	
Telephone	
Address	
City, State ZIP	

☐ **Credit Card**   ☐ **Check / Money Order**

Credit Card Number	
Expiration Date	
Signature	

Please Mail to: Book Jungle
PO Box 2226
Champaign, IL 61825
or Fax to: 630-214-0564

ORDERING INFORMATION

web: *www.bookjungle.com*
email: *sales@bookjungle.com*
fax: *630-214-0564*
mail: *Book Jungle PO Box 2226 Champaign, IL 61825*
or PayPal *to sales@bookjungle.com*

Please contact us for bulk discounts

DIRECT-ORDER TERMS

**20% Discount if You Order
Two or More Books**
Free Domestic Shipping!
Accepted: Master Card, Visa,
Discover, American Express

www.ingramcontent.com/pod-product-compliance
Lightning Source LLC
Chambersburg PA
CBHW081158170626
46813CB00009B/3243